Taking Time
for Me

Golden Age Books

Perspectives on Aging

Series Editor: Steven L. Mitchell

Taking Time for Me

How Caregivers Can Effectively Deal with Stress

Katherine L. Karr

Golden Age Books

PROMETHEUS BOOKS
Buffalo, New York

The mandalas positioned opposite various of the chapter title pages are circular symbols used throughout the ages by various cultures to designate wholeness. The mandalas found in this book were created by the caregivers as an art activity to help them express their inner strength.

Published 1992 by Prometheus Books

Photography by Katherine L. Karr

96 95 94 93 92   5 4 3 2 1

Library of Congress Cataloging-in-Publication Data

Karr, Katherine.
    Taking time for me : how caregivers can effectively deal with stress / by Katherine L. Karr.
        p.   cm.—(Golden age books)
    Inclues bibliographical references.
    ISBN 0-87975-779-5 (acid-free cloth)
    ISBN 0-87975-796-5 (acid-free paper)
    1. Aged—Care—United States. 2. Caregivers—United States—Psychology. 3. Stress management—United States. I. Title. II. Series.
HV1461.K36   1992
362.6—dc20   92-37600
                                                                    CIP

Printed in the United States on acid-free paper.

Contents

6   Contents

1

The Journey Begins

"What do you do to escape?"

The plea in Marlene's voice is unmistakable as she searches through her caregiver support group with a look of desperation in her eyes. Marlene is one of the group's y ongest members. Her husband had been diagnosed with inoperable, terminal cancer in the prime of his career. Six months later, ravaged by the disease, he was being nursed by Marlene around the clock. Having enlisted the aid of home hospice, she struggles to keep life manageable in the face of physical, mental, and emotional turmoil.

Her plea-filled question is met with awkward silence. Marlene persists: "Escape. You know. How do you get out from under it all . . . just long enough to get a piece of your sanity back?"

A throat is nervously cleared. Eyes look away. Hands shift in laps. Members of the group appear embarrassed to admit they are short on "escapes" themselves.

Marlene is not alone in her plea. She speaks for most of us who are caregivers. Many of us, however, do not have a supportive community to hear our plea. Marlene does.

Every week, in a comfortable room made available by a local church, Marlene and other Portland, Oregon, family caregivers gather to talk out their frustrations, share resources, and obtain the understanding and appreciation so necessary for those of us who put our lives in service to others. Like most caregivers, these men and women are doing an admirable job of taking care of their infirm family members. They recognize, however, that they are not taking as good care of themselves.

Few of us who are caregivers do. That fact comes as no surprise given the kind of stressors to which we are routinely subject:

- the physical strains of meeting another's needs for help in the daily activities of living;

- the multiple, seemingly endless demands on time, energy, and money;

- the loneliness and isolation of the job;

- the inability to structure time for oneself in the face of continuous demands;

- family misunderstandings and frictions;

- loss of privacy;

- loss of friends and social contacts;

- the emotional strain of living in an atmosphere of sickness, decline, impending death;

- the deadening weight of days, months, years, filled with arduous, repetitious responsibilities for which there can often be no thanks or appreciation;

- being the recipient of the anger and hostile behaviors which dependency behaviors can create and/or the abusive and erratic behaviors caused by brain damage in infirm family members.

Given such inevitable and ongoing stresses, why would so many of us willingly take on such an onerous job? Yet, most of us do it gladly, would not relinquish our duties, and are the last to be heard complaining publicly about the difficulties we must face.

"Come around after dark and peek through our blinds," jokes Sylvia, one of the Portland caregiver group, when a guest speaker comments on the composure of those gathered. "We're all great at appearances . . . when we're in public with our nonsmearable, tear-proof makeup on."

Sylvia is the one of the group who is always able to turn the bleakest of situations into a laughable one. "If I couldn't laugh," she once admitted to the group, "I would wash away in tears."

It seems Sylvia's brain damaged husband, unable to view life from

any positive perspective, not only demands much from Sylvia but is unable to know who she is or to offer any kind affirmation, much less affection. Knowing organic impairment causes his behavior does not make it easier to bear up under the unrelenting attacks.

"I'm a battered wife," she shares, half in jest. "Every day of my life in the face of continual haranguing and criticizing from my husband, I have to remind myself I *am* worthy, I *am* decent, I *am* a valuable human being; and above all, I *must* keep my sense of humor if I am going to survive."

Those of us who are caregivers likewise struggle to find ways to continue on with all-consuming and often discouraging responsibilities.

The struggle can be fierce.

The personal cost caregiving exacts is unusually high: Energy depletion and the physical strains of caregiving place our health at risk. The emotional strains, depression, discouragement, anger, frustration, guilt, and despair threaten our mental health. We want to provide family members with competent, comforting, compassionate care. Too often we fail.

Caregiving, more frequently than not, becomes a desperate attempt to maintain equilibrium while battling self-pity and petty behaviors of which we are not proud. We recognize that we must take better care of ourselves, but few of us have an actual program in place for doing so.

Generally speaking, we take better care of our family members than we do of ourselves.

Sometimes we have no choice in the matter. There are times when the day-to-day demands of caregiving force us to sacrifice our own needs for rest and relaxation.

Lack of time, however, is not the primary reason cited by most caregivers for failing to take better care of themselves. The reason is *lack of support and encouragement to do so.*

Human misery is not always solvable, but it is bearable. It is bearable when others are near to share the load and it is bearable when others shoulder our burdens until we can once again stand upright on our own accord.

Unfortunately, family caregiving is noted for its estranging nature. As demands mount, increasingly we find ourselves isolated from friends, neighbors, and all manner of former affiliations. Time does not permit much social outreach on our part. Friends and acquaintances often skirt close contact, finding themselves awkward around or repelled by disability, chronic illness, and impending death.

Left to ourselves, we find it difficult to muster the energy and motivation to put ourselves first. Nobody else does.

"I'll tell you about an escape my daughter planned for me that I will always remember." Marie turns to Marlene, breaking the silence.

"I took a respite vacation and flew back to the East Coast to visit her and her family. When I got off the plane, she whisked me to her spa where she had arranged for me to have an hour's massage. She said she wanted me to start my visit rested and relaxed."

An appreciative murmur echoes through the group.

"It was the first time in my entire life I had had a massage," Marie continues. "I would never have believed how absolutely wonderful and relaxed it made me feel. All the tensions I had been carrying around for weeks just seemed to melt away. I resolved on the spot as soon as I got back to Portland that I would find a masseuse and see her as regularly as I could."

"Are you?" several voices ask simultaneously.

"Funny thing . . ." Marie's voice trails off. "I came home and got all caught up in my customary caregiving routines and never have."

"But why not?" one of the group members persists. "You found out what a big help massage could be."

Marie shrugs. "I guess I'm just used to falling into that old caregiver trap: taking better care of my husband than I do of myself."

Marie's story makes it appear as though the failure is hers. It's not. If her daughter lived close by and provided the support, encouragement, and respite care enabling her mother to receive massage on a regular basis, Marie would be doing so.

Support is not a luxury. Support is necessary for survival.

We have not evolved as solitary creatures. In early societies the survival of an individual depended very much on the survival of the group. By supporting one another and staying intact, the group could hunt, gather food, build shelters, and defend itself far better than individuals could do on their own. Species survival was dependent upon interwoven systems of care, support, and protection.

Promoting one another's welfare is an integral part of human behavior because it has survival value.

In industrialized nations, we no longer need to rely on one another to sustain physical well-being. We maintain ourselves and our families without the interlocking support systems crucial to our earlier ancestors. Support for survival has changed in degree, not in kind. It has now become crucial for emotional well-being. Particularly for caregivers.

We do not fare very well without it. Study after study reveals that the most pervasive and severe consequencs of family caregiving, given its isolating and consuming nature, is in the realm of emotional distress. A long litany of mental health symptoms: depression, anxiety, helplessness, lowered morale, and chronic anger are found consistently among caregivers.[1]

It takes an exceptional person to labor day in and day out under the emotional duress of caregiving and not to succumb. Most of us do succumb, endangering both our physical and mental health.

"My husband will never again be the man I married," Sylvia tells the group. "His brain damage is irreversible. I live with a stranger; an angry, scornful, abusive stranger. And what is worse is that there is no end in sight for me; his physical health is excellent; he could live for years. The last ten years have been harder than anything I could have imagined, but it's worse knowing all I have to look forward to is another ten or twenty of those years . . . unless I'm carried out before he is. And at the rate I am going, I may be!"

Sylvia has a legitimate right to be angry, frustrated, and discouraged. In a very real way, she is victimized by her husband's condition, a condition she did not cause, a condition she is powerless to change.

Human beings were not made to go it alone under such conditions. Sylvia needs interlocking support systems just as our ancestors did. *Ideally,* her modern-day support system would include: immediate and extended family, friends, acquaintances, social service agencies, physicians, visiting nurses and social workers, an elder-care attorney, respite care workers, a church or synagogue community if appropriate, a support group, advocacy organizations such as the Alzheimer's Association, and other advocates knowledgeable about cutting through the bureaucratic red tape on her behalf when need be. Also included would be the public at large, standing ever ready to applaud and appreciate her efforts.

But the ideal is not the real. Contemporary social values do not regard family caregiving to be as socially redeeming as gainful employment, creative/artistic pursuits, or volunteerism. Nor is government particularly responsive to the billions of dollars spent yearly in service delivery by the informal network of family caregivers (between nine and eighteen billion dollars[2]). The insurance industry and the federal government, lobbied by physicians and the hospital industry, decided thirty years ago to pay hundreds of billions of dollars a year for the care of the dying in hospitals and long-term care facilities, while providing nothing for home custodial care.

Little has changed over the years. While respite hours are now available through Medicare benefits, they are limited to the medicare hospice portion of the benefit and a few demonstration projects. State and local government agencies have respite care programs available through in-home support services. Most, however, are on a sliding scale basis and have waiting lists and/or restrictive eligibility requirements. In some states, only those seniors with no family caregiver in the home are able to qualify for services.

We are left mostly to go it alone, and we do so to the best of our abilities. But for most of us, our caregiving will be flawed. It is flawed because we are too often tired, isolated, and emotionally bereft to be all that we would like to be. That does not mean we are unsuited to be caregivers. We become caregivers precisely because we are most apt to be persons with ample amounts of compassion, concern, and empathy; a strong sense of responsibility; and a ready willingness to place another's needs before our own.

Caring, however, is more than an *attribute* of personality. Caring is a *relational* experience. To nurture others, we need nurturance in return. Care has a reciprocal component. To give abundant care in a relationship and receive minimal or no care in return does not provide sufficient replenishment to allow us to continue quality caregiving; we simply get used up. With little coming back, there is less and less of us to give out. Feelings of bankruptcy set in. The stage is set for anger, frustration, and depression; all the emotional ills which beset caregivers.

Infirm family members are unlikely to be able to uphold their part of the caregiving relationship, for very understandable reasons. The caring relationship involving a sick or needy person is, by its very nature, going to be unequal. If, then, we are largely unable to obtain support from family and friends and only minimally, if at all, from the one for whom we care, we have to learn, along with Marlene, to nurture ourselves.

"I don't know why we are doing such a lousy job of talking about escapes," Don says as he suddenly comes to life in the group. "We all have them, healthy or unhealthy as they may be." A large box of donuts is being shared among group members.

"I'm not going to talk about my unhealthy ones, but for sure I couldn't hold up without this group and my tennis games. Mysteries

help a lot, too. I escape almost every night by losing myself in a good who-done-it."

There are murmurs of acknowledgment in the room. Don is not the only avid mystery reader.

"You read a lot?" Marlene inquires. Don nods.

"Then maybe you know some good books about reducing stress?"

"No." Don's reply comes back resoundingly. "I never read the heavy stuff. I'll stick with violence, lust, and suspense any old day!"

Liberal doses of mystery and suspense *would* make a more enticing book on stress. Even so, Don still might not read it. Of the group, he has the most committed and effective personal stress reduction program; rigorous physical exercise coupled with hobbies and mystery reading help keep his stress in check.

Don *has* to take care of himself. He has no immediate family within hundreds of miles. So demanding are his caregiving responsibilities, there would be nothing left to give out had he not learned the importance of daily replenishment.

Equally important is his reliance on group support. The most regular in attendance of the group's members, Don has been with the group since its inception some eighteen months ago. Few of his friends are able to give him the understanding, encouragement, and appreciation which he, like all caregivers, needs so desperately. For emotional support, he turns to fellow caregivers.

How can we caregivers likewise keep from feeling bankrupt and becoming prey to emotional stress? Learn the art of self-care. Take time for renewal activities guaranteed to relax, strengthen, and replenish.

Identify sources of support. Take time for them on a regular basis. Make them a high priority, even if that means starting a group from scratch with the help of a neighboring church or community center.

In emphasizing the importance of supportive communities this volume recognizes that not all of us may need to avail ourselves of support groups and/or encourage their formation. There will always be those who are able to derive all the help and emotional support they need from family, friends, neighbors, and membership in churches or other affinity groups. However, this group remains in the minority.

For that reason we focus on both the need for supportive communities and personal renewal. One without the other will be inadequate for the majority of persons who place their lives in service of another.

There is, of course, no "right" way to take time for ourselves. Renewal activities will remain as many and as varied as the people who employ them. This book is not written to be a compilation of renewal techniques. It is written to show how various methods of renewal serve as worthy deterrents to stress, as seen first-hand through the lives of caregivers who recognize that "taking time for me" must be the foundation of quality caregiving.

The caregivers whose stories are integral to this book do not claim to have totally succeeded in their efforts to better care for themselves. Most still have to work at making their own needs an ongoing priority. Like the majority of those who elect to give care, all have a long history of putting their needs last and are still having to learn to put their needs first on a regular basis.

None of the caregivers you will meet are novices at caregiving. Most have been at their jobs long, arduous years. They have many successes behind them; they have many failures. Experience has taught them to keep picking themselves up each time they falter, and when the going gets especially rough, they have one another's steadying hands to grasp.

Many persons would recoil from opening their private lives to public scrutiny. Not so with this group. They welcome their interactions and their stories being shared; for purposes of education, for purposes of inspiration, for purposes of empowerment. That is because they are *caregivers,* reaching out to others in their stock and trade.

"Hugs! Dear God we need them. Come on. Make it fast, but make it good!"

The hands of the clock point to two-thirty. Time for the group to break up, return home, and take up their posts.

It is Marie up on her feet, beckoning.

"You know what my life is about. I won't get another chance to be hugged for two whole weeks until I come back here!"

Marie speaks not only for herself. There is no hesitancy about entering the hugging circle. Eleven caregivers know what they need. Eleven caregivers know how to get it.

The hugging is close. The hugging is tight.

NOTES

1. Elizabeth Brody, "Parent Care as a Normative Family Stress," *The Gerontologist* 25, no. 1 (1985): 19–28.

2. Tish Sommers, *Women Take Care* (Gainesville, Fla.: Triad Publishing, 1987).

2

Don Holeman

The Importance of Exercise

"I started playing tennis when I was fourteen, pulled back on it for about 25 years because of the long hours I had to put in on my job, and then took it up again just about 20 years ago. That was when my wife's symptoms of multiple sclerosis began to manifest with greater seriousness. Increasingly my life revolved around caregiving. Eventually I had to take early retirement so I could have the time to do everything that needed to be done.

"Thankfully, I had tennis to fall back on. I don't know of a better way to release tension and stress. Every week I bat out the frustrations that are my constant companions.

"The local tennis club facility where I play sponsors a seniors program with a membership of 103 men and women. At seventy-three, I'm one of the oldest, but I'll tell you truthfully, after a two-hour session with a three-minute break every half hour, I could easily keep on playing. Someday they are going to carry me off the court on a stretcher, but what better way to go!

"If I didn't play tennis regularly and walk at least a mile a day my body wouldn't feel right, and that would add to my stress. I'm not sure what other caregivers do who don't get exercise, but they couldn't feel very good. I know it's easier to eat out frustration or watch television than to move your body, but that doesn't work for me. I have to move. My sanity is tied up in it.

"Of course, I've always been blessed with good health. I don't get even minor illnesses. When I had cataract surgery four years ago, the anesthesiologist asked me about the different medications I took. When I replied 'only an occasional aspirin,' he accused me of being a liar!

"Besides tennis, there is another way I have found to help me cope: model boat building. Right now I am building a radio controlled two-masted sailing schooner. Even the sails are radio controlled. It will take about 500 hours to complete. I try to spend at least two hours building every other day; at that rate I should have it completed in about ten months.

"If I could spend more time working on the boat, I would. But I can't. I have the full responsibility for the house, the yard, the grocery shopping, the meal preparation, my wife's personal needs . . . all of it!

"I would like to get away for a week or two. I have standing invitations from friends and family members who live in Hawaii, Arizona, and California. But in my situation, it is simply impossible. And I have had to come to accept that. What it's made me even more convinced of, though, is that if caregivers can't get two or three days off regularly from their responsibilities, they had better find ways each and every day to get out from under the stress.

"Because I can't get away, tennis, walking, and model building are my lifelines. The caregiver support group helps, too. You have to know there are people out there who understand your situation and are there to listen and help. It's just a shame none of them can play tennis or go walking with me!"

Lean, trim, physically fit for his seventy-three years, no one on first meeting would guess the caregiver burdens Don shoulders, day-in and day-out. Tennis and walking may *well* be his lifeline.

Although much of Don's caregiver stress is unrelenting, he can work off a certain amount of it; on the courts, on his daily walk. In the process of doing so, he strengthens his cardiovascular and respiratory systems, increasing the oxygen supply to his tissues and organs. His body's resilience is enhanced, and his blood pressure stays within acceptable limits, a feat often difficult for caregivers because of the intense strains inherent in the role.

Don differs from many other caregivers in that he has always liked playing his sport. Exercise is not a chore for him. Blessed with good health, he has long emphasized fitness as part of his lifestyle. If Don were out of shape or unused to exercise, it most likely would be difficult to convert to a program that requires a reasonably high level of motivation and a commitment to exercise, even when he is tired and worn from his responsibilities.

Although Don's exercise program is unlikely to be a model for most other caregivers, it illustrates several important points about exercise relative to those of us who want to do better by our bodies.

Don has elected a sport he can enjoy in conjunction with others.

Exercising with others is a wise choice for those who give care. Doing so carries a double payoff. We get the benefits of exercise along with the opportunity to be with others. A tennis club, a walking partner, a swimming group, a dancing class all can provide necessary companionship otherwise so difficult for many of us to come by.

Motivation is also increased when exercising with friends or through a class. With so many demands on our time, exercise can easily get shuffled. Then too, caregiving responsibilities have a way of draining away the very energy we need to exercise. When a commitment has been made to friends or a class, however, there is less likelihood of failing to follow through.

Don genuinely enjoys his chosen sport.

Even if Don only had a backboard to play against, he would probably still play tennis. On the other hand, he has no interest or enthusiasm for racquetball. If racquetball had to be his chosen form of exercise, working out would become a *duty,* not a pleasure. He would not continue to play.

An exercise program must be enjoyable if it is going to be effective and ongoing. Once it becomes an obligation, resistance sets in. Two words are fatal to an exercise program: I MUST.

Exercise gives Don a feeling of control over his life.

Like most people who give care, there is much in Don's life over which he has *no* control. He has duties and obligations whether he wants them or not. The vast majority of his time is not his own; it must be placed in service to his wife's needs and maintaining the household. The future is not his to plan; his wife's debilitating illness will largely dictate what the future holds for them both.

What Don *does* control is his body: by choosing to keep fit and healthy, not only does he feel good, he looks good. He is toned and trim; he has a good self-image. The feelings of futility, despair, and frustration common to all caregivers still plague him. But exercise helps keep him resilient. He has an outlet for stress, and he uses it. Mastery for Don is bouncing back. He has good reason to feel in control.

Exercise affords Don an overall sense of physical well-being.

Don's body not only feels healthier as a result of exercise, it *is* healthier.

When we don't exercise regularly, we adapt to low demands on our cardiovascular system. Our heart and lungs provide less oxygenated blood to our muscles, and they weaken. We tire more easily and are not able to accomplish all we would like. Don's regular exercise has increased the circulation to his organs and tissues. When walking or playing tennis, his muscles set up rhythmic contractions, pumping a rich supply of blood from his heart to his lungs. As a result, he has the energy and stamina that accompany a well-functioning cardiovascular system.

Tennis playing and walking also enable Don to work off considerable amounts of stress. Anytime bodies encounter stressful situations, they secrete chemical agents known as catechalamines, adrenalin-like substances that cause nervousness and edginess. A brisk walk or other form of exercise helps the body reabsorb these chemicals, thereby reducing tension and strain.[1]

Exercise also helps to increase the blood level of endorphins, opiate-like molecules produced by the brain. Unlike catechalamines, these chemical agents have a beneficial effect, giving a sense of well-being that exercise physiologists refer to as a "natural high."[2]

Don may not understand all the physiology involved in explaining why exercising makes him feel good. He does not need to. The good feelings themselves are sufficient reward.

Regularity is the key to Don's exercise program.

Don goes to the tennis courts weekly, playing two hours at a stretch. His walks are daily. He knows that to reap the rewards of exercise, it must be regular and ongoing.

Most of us know exercise is good for us; most know what form of exercise we prefer. But unless we exercise on a regular basis, the benefits of exercise will be lost.

It takes resolve to exercise, and resistance to ignore the voice in our head which tries to tell us we can get by just fine without exercise. It is the voice of our lazy self, the part of us aligned with the principle of inertia. There are two ways to deal with the voice: ignore it, or refute it.

Don's exercise is rigorous for a man of his age. But it's not necessary to take up tennis to reap the benefits of exercise. Increasingly, studies confirm that persons who engage in moderate exercise for thirty minutes daily, whether it be as walking or gardening, receive most of the health benefits of those who engage in more rigorous pursuits.

In a more disturbing vein, the same studies reveal that persons who are sedentary do not live as long as their more active counterparts; nor is their health as good. By not exercising, we are making a choice, one that puts our health at risk.

The more at risk we become, the more our bodies give out warning signals. Among them are the following:

- shortness of breath after negotiating stairs; or after short periods of exertion;

- difficulty sleeping;

- poor circulation: cold hands, cold feet, bluish nails;

- muscle tension;

- obesity;

- flabby skin, poor muscle tone;

- general tiredness, fatigue, boredom;

- high blood pressure.

Don does not exhibit any of those symptoms. If any of us do, it would be well to seek out a physician who understands the role of exercise and diet in maintaining health.

Walking is the exercise that best suits Don's caregiver lifestyle.

If there is an exercise particularly suited to caregivers, it would have to be walking. Many of us may not be able to get away on a regular basis to golf, swim, or play tennis, but most of us *can* shut the door behind on responsibilities to go walking, however briefly. Just two fifteen minute walks daily can provide important health benefits, while helping us free up from strain.

Our bodies are built for walking. When we habitually sit, stand, or lie down, blood pools in our lower extremities; muscles and bones can begin to atrophy. But when we walk, our bodies turn into dynamic exercise machines that make use of almost all our muscles and bones.

With one single synchronized movement, walking exercises more of the body including lungs and heart than any other activity. Stresses and injuries, which can occur with other exercises or sports, are practically nonexistent with walking. Recognized to be the safest of the aerobic exercises, walking gives all the cardiovascular training effects produced by running, jumping, and aerobic dancing but with none of the injuries.

Don does not do aerobic, power, or race walking. Even a moderately paced walk improves circulation, burns calories, and activates a continuous rhythmic movement of all the major muscle groups, while giving the psychological boost of getting outside the confines of the caregiving environment.

Don's commitment to exercise provides many useful pointers. But since he is long years into his regime, there are two additional points to make for caregivers who are or will be at the beginning stages of exercise. Those who are newly contemplating an exercise commitment should pay close attention to events which reward or punish the activity.

- Recognize and expect some discomfort. Muscles not accustomed to being used are likely to ache. Walking even a half mile at a steady pace may be exhausting. *It is important not to focus on the discomforts.* They soon pass as strength and endurance build and as flexibility increases with the repeated use of muscles. A warm bath and aspirin will take care of most discomfort.

- Realize that there will be a greater likelihood of giving up if family members are unsupportive or critical. *It takes strengthened resolve to maintain commitment in the face of disparagement.* On the other hand, support and encouragement from others will be of enormous help, particularly in the beginning stages when exercise can be more tiring than pleasureable. Once exercise becomes regular and ongoing, and we have reached the point of feeling good physically and mentally, days *without* exercise feel empty. And even if others are not supportive, the chances of abandoning our commitment will be highly unlikely.

- We must care about ourselves and our bodies or no exercise program can be successful. Unless we value ourselves, there will be no motivation to take care of our bodies. The human body is a superb piece of engineering. The better we take care of it, the better it will take care of us, but to do so, the care has to be genuine.

Is it ever too late to begin exercising? No. In a nationally acclaimed study, a highly respected physician, Dr. Dean Ornish, specializing in heart problems, conducted pioneering research to halt or reverse heart disease in coronary patients. He did so without bypass surgery, angioplasties, or cholesterol lowering drugs. The core of his program was exercise, dietary changes, stress management techniques, and group support.[3] The study demonstrated that no matter how out-of-condition people get, their bodies are amazingly resilient. All of us can reverse the damage we have done to ourselves as a result of stress, poor diet, lack of exercise, and unhealthy lifestyles.

So why aren't we all exercising? Because we can never know the benefits of exercise until we actually do it and do it regularly. Exercise itself is never the problem. The problem lies in unwillingness to make the *effort* to exercise. Considerable resolve is necessary to persevere with an activity whose benefits may not be immediate, particularly when the more out-of-shape we are, the harder the initial stages will be.

No one can give resolve to another. Resolve comes from within. Self-discipline and fortitude do not come easily when we are tired and well acquainted with despair. But somewhere deep inside every caregiver is a fighting spirit. It keeps us fighting to do what is just and right for our infirm family member, even when society will not do its share. It keeps us fighting to meet the exacting care needs of a loved one regardless of the cost to ourselves.

The same fighting spirit needs to be (and can be) turned toward ourselves to work on our behalf if we will but give it a chance. We *can* begin walking on a regular basis. We *can* persevere with a water exercise class. It may not be easy at first, but then, we have a track record of not giving up. So why give up on caring for ourselves? Bodies exercised and cared for are responsive and give back with increased stamina, an enhanced self-image, a feeling of being in control, and a greater overall sense of well-being. What better and more important gift could we give to ourselves, all for the price of resolve?

Don says he won't stop playing tennis until they carry him off the courts on a stretcher. For a man in his seventies, that's not stupidity, that's fighting spirit. The same fighting spirit is in all of us if we will but give it a chance!

NOTES

1. Mike Samuels, *The Well Adult, A Complete Guide to Improving Your Health* (New York: Summit Books, 1988).

2. Ann Kashiwa, *Fitness Walking for Women* (New York: Putnam Publishing Group, 1987).

3. Dean Ornish, M.D., *Dr. Dean Ornish's Program for Reversing Heart Disease* (New York: Random House, 1990).

3

The Case for Solidarity

"Why can't people learn from the cranes!" exclaims Helen, after hearing a group member share an inspiring account about the big birds.

Cranes, it seems, often group together for support, taking turns playing the leader. When they are flying together and one begins tiring, the others gather around to help, lift, and encourage. Cranes appear to be naturally cooperative birds, which may be why, in the East, they are the symbol of longevity.

Helen has just returned to the Portland group after a long absence necessitated by complications in her husband's care. For three months, there have been a series of breakdowns in his care delivery systems, leaving Helen frustrated, isolated, and heavily burdened.

Cranes are not on the endangered species list. Nor are caregivers, at least not yet. We may be in the not-so-distant future if we don't do a better job of getting our needs met.

In March of 1992, a Portland, Oregon, Alzheimer's patient made national headlines when he was found abandoned at an Idaho race track. The circumstances surrounding his particular abandonment were both crass and disgraceful. The incident brought to the public's attention the seventy thousand other frail elders who are abandoned yearly, most under very temporary and far less conniving conditions. The number is expected to increase.

Caregivers reading the statistics recognize unreported stories, which are less about abandonments and more about caregivers reaching their limits of endurance. Exhaustion, frustration, anger, and despair drive most of us from time-to-time to caregiving behaviors of which we are not proud. Abandonment occurs when those behaviors are carried to extremes. Most caregivers who are guilty of abandonment are not irresponsible; they are unable to get their own needs met.

Caregivers are at risk and we need to admit it. We need to make serious and committed efforts to meet our needs, individually *and* collectively. Elder abandoment is too blatant a symptom of caregiver stress to be ignored.

"I don't know what's wrong with me," blurts out a caregiver on her first visit to the group. "I am almost chronically angry. I shouldn't be that way. My husband can't help what is happening to him. But I have almost no time to myself now. I'm on edge all the time. I work to keep from screaming. More and more I am failing."

"You've come to the right place," Bea responds. "Believe me, we all know exactly what you're talking about."

If availability of support services are any indication of society's sensitivity to caregivers' needs, it must be said that society has chosen to remain largely insensitive. Policy experts know a great deal about who we are but very little about what we need.

By the year 2000 there will be some ten million elderly persons in the United States who will need help with day-to-day tasks of food preparation, dressing, and bathing. This rate will have *doubled* since 1985.[1]

Contrary to popular belief, the majority of infirm elderly never have or never will be living in nursing homes. Even when they are disabled or ill enough to qualify for institutional care, most older persons are still cared for within their communities. Some hire private homemaker and nursing services enabling them to remain on their own; some receive services funded by governments or private charities. But the vast majority, between 80 and 90 percent, are cared for by family members.[2]

Who are we—those of us who provide family caregiving? Mostly we are older women. If we care for our husbands, our average age is sixty-five, but 30 percent of us are over seventy-four. Those of us who are daughters are most likely to be over fifty.[3]

Our health and financial status is poor. A third of us are at poverty level; almost half of us are in poor health, mostly because we are older ourselves. Yet the amount of care we provide is staggering, with 30 to 40 percent of us working far in excess of our normal household duties. Caregiving for the majority in our ranks is the equivalent of a full-time job, which is why many of us give up our outside employment to care for our relatives. It is not unusual for the "new" job to be around the clock.[4]

It does not take a statistician to realize there are millions of caregivers putting in billions of hours of care, year in and year out.

But this is not the whole story. Missing is how caregiving adversely affects our lives if we fail to get the renewal, time off, and help that we need. Missing is what happens when, unlike cranes, we find no one near to lift and encourage us when we falter. Only headlines tell the story. After we falter. After the fact.

"I come here," says Bea, "because it is the only place I get help and feel understood. No one else wants to really hear about what I'm going through. I never thought I would feel so utterly alone. I would never have believed I would come back each evening from my husband's nursing home hoping against hope to see the light on my telephone answering machine blinking. That way, I would at least know someone had been thinking about me enough to call or want to be of help."

Loneliness and isolation have disturbing consequences for those who do not purposely choose them—particularly caregivers. Faced with problem situations that can deny us satisfying involvements with extended family, neighborhoods, work environments, and social interaction, our focus becomes more exclusively on ourselves. Worry, cynicism, negativity, and depression intensify. So does chronic stress. So do self-destructive habit patterns such as overindulgence and drug use.

On the one hand, studies continue to document the absolute importance of social relations for health. Persons who are isolated have a two- to threefold increased risk of death over those who feel most connected to others.[5] On the other hand, being an attending member of a church or synagogue, or having a significant group involvement, protects people from heart disease—even when they have high blood pressure—and lessens the risk of premature death.[6]

Why do we need one another? It cannot be said too many times: FOR SURVIVAL. Intimacy is healing. Isolation is killing.

Reviewing mounting evidence that social isolation heightens people's susceptibility to illness, *Science Magazine* concludes:

"It's the 10-20 percent of people who say they have no one with whom they can share their private feelings or who have close contact with others *less* than once a week who are the most at risk. Social isolation is as significant to mortality rates as are all the other predictors of death: namely, high blood pressure, smoking, high cholesterol, obesity, and lack of physical exercise. Those with few or weak social ties are *twice* as likely to die as those with strong social ties."[7]

"My family and friends are always telling me what a great job I'm doing." There is an edge in Marie's voice. **"They compliment me on being so strong and persevering. Well, I'm sick of having to be strong. I hate being strong. I want to be weak for a change. I want to be the one cared for."**

Where did we ever get the idea we could go it alone? From our conditioning. From being part of a fiercely individualistic ethic. From living in a white, Anglo-Saxon, secular culture that holds individuals up to be isolated and strong unto themselves.

Were we living in other cultures, the encouragement, the understanding, the support we need would be supplied by our kinship system, friends, and interlocking community network system. These are the cultures far less individually centered than ours. Strength is drawn from the cohesiveness of the community.

Not so in the United States. Other than their caregiver's group, few of the members have someone they can lean upon. As members are quick to point out, it is not unusual to find close neighbors, a church community, and even family members impervious to the fact that a fellow human being is overwhelmed by responsibilities and would benefit enormously from some care and concern.

Modern individualism has grown at the expense of civic and biblical traditions. It has pursued individual rights and individual autonomy in ever-widening realms. But whereas an absolute commitment to individual dignity has corrected the inequities which existed between husbands and wives, masters and servants, leaders and followers, haves and have nots, it has violated those of our country's founding traditions that sustained genuine individuality while *simultaneously* nurturing integrated community life.

Be strong. Be self-reliant. Be sufficient unto yourself. These are the societal messages, drilled into us from childhood on. Conditioning is subtle and complex involving the models to which we are exposed, the literature we read, and the media from which we take our messages.

Seated around the radio listening to "The Lone Ranger" or watching Scarlett O'Hara on the big screen, reading Charlotte Brontë, Jane Austin, Virginia Woolf, Mark Twain, Nathaniel Hawthorne, and Ernest Hemingway, Marie grew up learning that if she were to succeed at any undertaking, it would be because *Marie* triumphed, *Marie* overcame all odds, *Marie's* stiff upper lip held.

Newer books are in fashion. Television has replaced radio as the major agent of aculturation. But each generation has its share of popular heroes and heroines who demonstrate the virtue of self-reliance. If mysteries are good "escape" reading, it may be partly because they champion the image of going it alone, which is exactly what most caregivers are forced to do. More than any other modern American hero, the hardboiled detective blends the ideal of moral courage with lonely individualism. From Sam Spade to Serpico, from Phillip Marlow to Travis McGee, the fierce independence of the detective is also his strength. Mysteries may well be escape reading but the message they convey is that to serve, we must stand alone, not need others, and engage in a kind of heroic selflessness, until we break.

"I'm getting so that I am not a very nice person to be around." The words come tumbling out. **"I'm short, I'm snappy, I'm petty. But then, everything I do is wrong in my husband's eyes. He doesn't let me out of his sight. His demands never end."** The new member gestures nervously.

"I'm nearing the end of my rope." Standing up, she shakes her fist . . . again, again, again, and then drops back on the davenport.

"How are you feeling right now?" Don inquires after a few moments of silence have elapsed.

"Actually, better." There is a long sigh. **"Ranting in front of people who can understand does get rid of a lot of frustration!"**

The room is filled with knowing laughter.

Individualism is not going to be our triumph, at least not those of us who are caregivers. Our strength is in relationships, support, and being there one for another. It's not strengthening to go it alone. It is weakening. And if there are no cultural models or modern-day heroes and heroines who teach us to rely on one another, then the burden rests squarely on us to be the teachers.

As caregivers, we must be seriously concerned about our own health and well-being. As *self-reliant* human beings, we must learn, each in our own way, how to keep ourselves healthy in mind, in body, and in spirit. But we also need to broaden our concerns about health and well-being to encompass other women and men who serve under similar conditions.

Partly because there is a lot in it for us: Personal dilemmas are more easily solvable when we don't have to go it alone, so stiffly upper-lipped. Taking greater responsibility for others gives our own lives deeper meaning than is possible when we focus exclusively on our own need base. Reaching out brings its own rewards; not selfishly, but deservedly. Those who become the new heroes and heroines will do so because they appreciate this fact and project solidarity rather than narrow self-reliance. They will recognize, as caregivers do, that we are all in this together. And like the cranes, we are only going to succeed in our endeavors to the extent we can stretch our wings . . . and our hearts . . . to one another.

"Give me a call on the days you have to struggle every minute to keep your chin up." Eilene turns to the caregiver on edge. "I know all about those days. I'll come over and help you. Or we will go out some place together. And don't think I am doing it just for you. I have to have someone besides my husband to take care of. I'm drying up with loneliness. He can't give anything back. You can!"

NOTES

1. Sommers, *Women Take Care.*
2. Ibid.
3. Ibid.
4. Ibid.
5. Ornish, *Dr. Dean Ornish's Program for Reversing Heart Disease.*
6. Ibid.
7. As reported in: Dean Ornish, M.D., "The Healing Power of Love," *Prevention Magazine* (February 1991): 60–66.

4

Helen Sandstrom

Overcoming Worry and Depression

"I'll tell you the most important thing—not giving in to your problems. If I let myself worry about all the things I have to worry about, well, I'd never get off this chair. But I don't let myself do that. As soon as I start feeling bad, I make myself get up and get moving.

"In the spring and summer there is always my garden to work in. I've been gardening since I was little, growing up on a farm in Italy. We had cows and chickens and raised all our own vegetables. They had to last us through the winter. We dried the corn and kept it in bins along with the chestnuts and potatoes. During the Depression here in America, we got by because we could grow all of our own food. I lived with my sister and brother-in-law; their income came from fattening hogs for market. We had enough land to grow everything we needed.

"After I married, my husband and I saved for years to buy some property of our own to build a home, this same one I still live in. The piece of property had been used as a garbage dump by the neighborhood. It looked awful, and took us two years to clear. We were too poor to hire any of it done; but at night, after my husband got home from his job, we would walk over to dig out the garbage and crab grass. When it got dark, the street lamp on the corner gave us enough light to keep working.

"The first thing we did when we got the lot looking respectable was to plant flowers: every kind imaginable: petunias, pansies, tulips, marigolds, hollyhocks, sweet peas, wallflowers. We had hundreds of flowers of every color. So beautiful! No one could have ever guessed that the lot was once a garbage dump. Next we put in the vegetables: corn, potatoes, carrots, beans. And *then* we were ready to start building our home!

"I am seventy-eight this year, and I still put in a garden. Nothing tastes as good as your own vegetables. I almost never have to go to the produce section in the grocery store when summer comes. The apple and cherry trees we planted still bear fruit. This year something is wrong with the cherry; I'm going to have to get out and spray it. Until last year I was able to mow the grass, too. Now it's too much for me, so I have a teenager do it. Working outside gets my mind off myself and my worries. All the things that depress me seem to go away when I start working in my yard.

"Being around people keeps my spirits up, too. My family has always been close. I wish I could see them more often. But I don't drive and neither does my sister, so it's hard to get together. Sometimes I get to take care of my two-year-old granddaughter. She can be a handful but I sure enjoy having her around. And then there is my church. I live close enough to walk to Mass and do things with the senior citizens group. When I can get a ride, I go to my caregiver support group.

"It's not that I don't get depressed. I do. And I cry real easily. But you have to decide whether you're going to let your problems get you down, or do something to stop dwelling on them. Often the evenings are the worst times for me. Things just have a way of closing in. But when they do, I usually make myself get up, go in the kitchen, and start baking something. Lots and lots of times I've made cookies and pastries late at night.

"I love to bake. You can't buy the good pastries you once could when they used real butter and fresh cream and eggs. Now you've got to make pastries yourself if they're going to taste right. My cholesterol is too high. The doctor doesn't want me eating eggs. I'm supposed to be cutting back on sweet things. But I cheat. I have to. I tell myself if I skip on the egg for breakfast, I can have a little piece of pie for lunch!

"Cooking relaxes me. It never is a chore. My husband sure likes my cooking. I take baking to him at the retirement home. As often as I can, I bring him home. I walk over; it's maybe a mile. Then we get on the bus to come back. The two blocks we have to walk when we get off give him some good exercise. He doesn't get much where he is, and he is starting to shuffle. I don't know how much longer I can get him on the bus.

"My husband is from German stock; he is very strong, very stubborn. Nine years ago he had a stroke while up on a ladder and fell down quite a ways. The doctors didn't expect him to live, he was hurt so bad. But he did live. After months in the hospital and in a rehabilitation unit he was able to come home. I took care of him for five years. Then he had a second stroke, and I just couldn't keep on with his care.

"The retirement home he is in is not far from here. That's why I can go get him on the bus. The problem is, they are really cutting corners to keep open. There is never enough staff to give the kind of attention the people really need. And if my husband gets so he can't walk or bathe himself, they won't keep him.

"Each time I bring him home, it seems like he's getting a little worse. And there is usually some kind of crisis: he falls or cannot get up out of the bathtub. I don't know how I get him up. I think I get a lot of strength from God because if I stay calm and say a little prayer, it just sort of comes to me what to do.

"But even though my faith really helps me, I still can't keep from worrying about what's ahead for both of us. Our savings are running low. I would hate to give up our home. There are such wonderful memories here. I have a closet full of photograph albums. I look at pictures of my family and remember all the happy times.

"It's good to have memories, a kitchen, a garden, and faith. Maybe it's kind of simple compared with what other people have. I guess everybody has problems any way you look at it. All I know is that mine don't seem so bad when I can make an apple pie with a real pastry crust from apples off our tree. And then sit back and watch my family enjoy it!"

Worry and depression are no more foreign to Helen than they are to others of us who give care. What makes Helen different, however, is that she consistently takes certain measures to keep them from getting her down. And although she may not know it, her measures are the very strategies mental health personnel recommend using when worry and depression threaten.

TAKE CONSTRUCTIVE ACTION

Recognizing constructive action counters worry and depression, Helen has learned to busy herself in her garden, her kitchen, or elsewhere about the house. Even if it is late at night, she gets up and begins to work in her kitchen rather than lie awake worrying. Long experience has taught her a fundamental mental health fact: *action is the natural enemy of depression.*

It is not that Helen is more disciplined than the rest of us. Often she has to force herself to take action. Worry and depression drain off energy. They make us tired and lethargic. When depression strikes, most of us don't even want to *think* about taking constructive action, much less make the effort to do so.

Helen is not unique in this regard. Many times she must struggle to push herself up from her chair. But as hard as that first push may be, it is usually sufficient to get her going. Once outdoors to pick a bouquet, she is likely to stay another hour weeding, keeping her worries at bay.

Cleaning the basement, changing oil in the car, scrubbing and waxing floors are not the most glamorous depression fighters, but they work. Action energizes; it gives a sense of accomplishment. Energy and accomplishment are enemies of depression. As long as we are willing to expend the effort to get the action started, depression will be a lot more apt to yield than if we refrain from taking action. It may take an extra cup of coffee or a pep talk from a friend to help us make that effort. It is not easy to control our moods. They like to have the upper hand. It is gratifying when we don't allow them to take command, and have something to show for it in the process. That is what Helen does. Her garden is weedless, and her worries have been banished.

EXERCISE

It helps Helen to keep on the move. She works in her yard. She walks to her husband's retirement home. She walks to her church. Walking and gardening give her relief from tension and worries.

In addition to the health benefits of exercise discussed in chapter 2, physical exertion gets Helen outside for fresh air and a change of scenery. Outdoor exercise is beneficial for almost everyone, regardless of age or life style. But when we are caring for an ill or disabled person, such a change, for however short a time, is particularly important. The atmosphere of sickness is depleting and depressing. Breaking away to do marketing and errands provides some relief but it does not give the health or psychological benefits of an energizing walk.

Endorphins, the brain chemicals generated through exercise, are known as our bodies' natural depression fighters. When we exercise, particularly outside, our biochemistry changes: moods lighten and attitudes become more positive. Sights and sounds of Nature combine with an altered body chemistry to restore confidence in our ability to cope. This is true of Helen and helps account for her commitment to walking as often as she can.

Rain or shine, garden or no garden, any of us can give our confidence level a similar boost, leaving worries to fend for themselves. Therapists need considerable education to become skilled in countering depression. We don't. We need a sturdy pair of walking shoes, an umbrella if need be, and the strength of will to close the door behind us.

CREATIVE ACTIVITIES

Creative talent is not reserved for artisans and musicians. Helen's creative abilities are in evidence each time she goes into the kitchen or garden to express herself uniquely in ways that give her joy.

Creative self-expression can take any number of forms. The form is less important than the expression in a manner that gives satisfaction, enjoyment, and a sense of fulfillment. Today it may mean hooking a rug. Tomorrow it may be an artful arrangement of photographs on poster board. Whatever form creative expression takes, it brings with it a form of liberation from the restrictions of caregiving and from the worries that plague those who care for others.

So much of our time must be spent in service to our family member that whole portions of our identity get submerged. Creative projects help to reclaim the parts of ourselves we put on hold.

Worrying about problems seldom, if ever, solves them. Being depressed about problems does not make them go away. If we need a focus for our minds, we might as well focus on something productive. For Helen, that may be making plum jelly with the right balance of sweetness and tartness. Others, weary of kitchen duty, will recoil from the thought of cooking as a means of creative expression. We may need to trouble shoot circuit boards, plot a children's story, or arrange pansies in pots.

Whatever form creative expression takes, it will succeed to the degree it gives us enjoyment. Helen's butter-flaked pastries bring a measure of joy to her life that might otherwise be missing. Maybe they do elevate her cholesterol level, but they also raise her happiness quotient. Her physician may not see the trade-off as a beneficial one, but those of us who give care know full well that it is.

GUARDING AGAINST ISOLATION

Although Helen's children and their families all live a distance from her, she is able to draw on support from them via long distance telephone calls and periodic visits. Her church and her caregiver support group fill some needs for companionship. However, most of the time that she is not with her husband is spent by herself. Worries and depression intensify in isolation. The isolating nature of the caregiver's job is more likely to be the cause of depression than is a disorder in personality.

A century ago, social welfare programs did not exist. Cures for many illnesses were unknown; acutely traumatic disease and unexpected deaths were the norm. Most people could not afford comforts on any scale; if crops failed or there was not work to be had, people could go hungry. And yet, a deeper connectedness to one another kept worries more manageable. Larger, closer family ties offered substantial emotional support, as did church and community ties. People prayed and played together; relationship and meaning was spread throughout the community. Not to have others close by to help share burdens was the exception, not the rule.

Although times have radically changed, our needs for one another have not. Relaxing, sharing, and just enjoying the company of others is like a transfusion for Helen; it is life-giving. In addition to the emotionally satisfying nature of human interaction, involvement with others allows her important self-confirmation. There are parts of Helen's personality that come into play primarily in the company of others, parts that help her feel good about herself. She needs to nurture and spoil others who are healthy and appreciative of her care, like her children and grandchildren. (Her husband cannot give her thanks or appreciation in his condition.) She has warmth and sympathy to share with others who are encountering trials and need to be comforted. This she can do with her caregiver group. Helen has a playful side that enjoys recreational activities and leisure time involvement with others. This she can find with her senior citizens church group.

Being in situations where we can activate those parts of ourselves that are not given much reign in the caregiver role is both affirming and vitalizing. Narrowness of focus invites worry and depression. To interpret isolation with meaningful experiences involving friends not only feeds us emotionally, it gives us the opportunity to be more of who we are. Health is a matter of completion, not fragmentation. While there are those who can be healthy and complete unto themselves, most of us cannot. Helen's family, caregiver friends, and church group allow her to give the gift of herself. They are the richer for it and so is she.

A COURSE OF ACTION FOR DOWN TIMES

Reminiscing is the course of action Helen pursues in down times. Knowing happy memories will dislodge worries, she gets out her photograph albums and begins reclaiming meaningful life events. Pictures trigger her imagination; she is flooded with images of special family times and occasions of joy. These years are difficult periods in her life; yet she is able to realize just how much life *has* been good to her; how much she has to be thankful for.

Gratitude is a strong antidote to unhappiness. When we are grateful for an experience, we feel delight, enjoyment, and appreciation while simultaneously recognizing the blessings and wonder of that moment.

Depression and worry have a fiendish way of making us resist feeling grateful. It is as though we have to train ourselves to counter such resistance by making a clear choice to be more aware of how much we really have been given. People once used communal celebrations to remember: religious services of thanksgiving, seasonal rituals, and the like. But because most of us seldom have the opportunity to express gratitude in any ongoing collective way, reminiscing can be our touchstone for expressing this thankfulness.

"Remember the pride we felt when. . . ."

"Remember when our good friend. . . ." .

"Remember the trip to. . . ."

"Remember when sickness was beaten back. . . ."

"Remember when. . . ."

In addition to rekindling happy memories in our hearts and serving as an inducement to gratitude, reminiscing also can help us call to mind times in the past when our courage and fortitude allowed us to weather life's difficulties. All of us, at some time in our lives, have had occasion when by will and determination we were able to gain greater mastery of life's challenges. Holding onto these memories can strengthen our confidence in our ability to handle difficulties in the present.

"Remember when our family member was hospitalized and we. . . ."

"Remember when it seemed the money wasn't going to stretch and. . . ."

"Remember when there seemed to be no way out, but we. . . ."

"Remember when. . . ."

Reminiscing is Helen's special course of action for down times. There are many others: inspirational aids*; long distance calls to caring relatives; relishing small and simple pleasures†; special places to visit— a favorite park, a shrine, a scenic secret of our own; a place where we are brought to peace . . . or joy.

Worry can be thought of as a spasm of the emotions; a condition where the mind clutches onto certain thoughts and will not release them. It doesn't help when people tell us we need to stop worrying; we cannot. Obsessional thoughts have us in their grip. Our job is not to "try" to stop worrying. Instead, we must substitute thoughts or actions to break the grip of worry.

That Helen has elected reminiscing as her course of action for down times is less important than the fact that she has a strategy in place. She *knows* what helps her when misery sets in—going through her photograph albums. Looking through the albums, however, is the easy part. The hard part is *making the effort to go and get them down.* It is no easier for Helen to push herself up from her chair when she is feeling depressed than it is for the rest of us. But she does and is always the better for it.

---

*See pages 152–153.
†See pages 169–170.

TAKE WORRY APART

Most worries never materialize. When and if they do come to pass, we generally find a way of handling them. We need the cold, factual eye of rational thought to put worries in perspective.

The stronger our emotional make-up, however, the more difficult it is to think rationally. Emotions are irrational occurrences. It is difficult to be coolly factual when we are seething with anger or churning with frustration. These are the very times most of us will benefit from the assistance of others who can help us detach from our emotions and our worries by examining them in a more rational light.

Gerontology workers, for example, could explain to Helen that she is in no danger of losing her home, no matter how strained family finances become. Oregon's Spousal Impoverishment Act allows assets to be divided before they are exhausted by the care needs of one of the partners.* Moreover, the State of Oregon will not allow any claims against her home from creditors until both she and her husband have died. Factual, rational information could set one of her worries permanently to rest.

Because most of Helen's family lives out of town and she only infrequently gets to her support group, she is not accustomed to taking her worries apart with others. Those of us more fortunate to have people available in whom we can confide need to add this approach to our list of coping strategies. It can be an amazingly quick way to set some worries permanently to rest.

Constructive action, exercise, creative projects, the company of others, courses of action for down times, and subjecting worry to rational scrutiny are not *cures* for worry and depression. They can, however, keep these two concerns from unduly ruling our lives.

The times when worry and depression do get the upper hand are usually the very times when, unlike Helen, we fail to rally against them. It may be that we have not understood how to go about helping ourselves. It may be that we have chosen not to make the effort to do so. And then again, it may be that we have not done so because something deep and forceful within will not allow us.

Over twenty million Americans suffer from more serious forms of chronic depression than does Helen. For some of them—and some

---

*Readers are encouraged to check the relevant legislation in their own state by contacting their local representatives.

of us are among them—self-help approaches do not suffice. The strategies elaborated upon above need always be the first line of attack. When, however, they fail in spite of our best efforts and desire, depression may be severe enough to warrant chemical intervention.

Caregiving is difficult enough without the complications of chronic depression. The more unrelenting depression is, the more it is likely to undermine the quality of our caregiving. Under such circumstances, not only do we owe it to ourselves to get professional help, we owe it to those who rely on us for care. Fortunately there are many new anti-depressants on the market that carry far fewer side effects or addictive properties than once was the case. Consultation with a trusted physician will determine which medications will be the most appropriate.

Helen does not need chemical intervention. She has found her own ways to wage the battle against worry and depression. Perhaps others can now do a better job of waging that battle themselves, with her guidelines giving clearer direction. Some of us, though, may not find her story directly applicable to our lives. It will seem easier for Helen to get on top of her worries because she has more time for herself, no longer being so consumed with her husband's home care. That well may be the case. But there is another part of Helen's story yet to be told. It is the part that *does* make her story applicable.

For three years after her husband's fall, Helen took care of him at home, managing in the way caregivers manage. Then came another seizure. This one paralyzed emotional centers in his left brain, leaving him with only negative emotions for perceiving his world. Overnight he became an angry, critical, embittered man. It was Helen who had to bear the brunt of his hostility.

Life with her husband quickly became a nightmare for Helen. Whatever she did was wrong in her husband's eyes. Depression, worry, and tears were her daily companions. Neurologists urged her to place her husband elsewhere at least two years before she could bring herself to do so. In the meanwhile, sanity for Helen became dependent upon the very strategies she uses today for fighting worry and depression.

In back of happiness usually lies conquered unhappiness. Conquered unhappiness is Helen's real story. Apple pies and marigolds are important but not its central theme. Helen's life displays the courage of a defiant caregiver who, when worry and depression crowd in, pushes herself up from her chair and goes resolutely to scout out the weeds in her garden, gets down her beloved photograph albums, or rolls out her butter-flaked pastries.

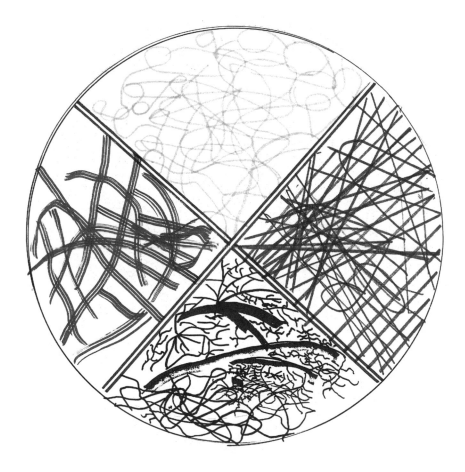

5

Taking Control of Stress

"At least three different times I made a concerted effort to get this woman to talk about *herself and her needs*. She could not do it." Barbara is describing a recent encounter she had with a caregiver who was not a part of the group.

"All she could talk about was her husband, his condition, and how he had changed over the course of his illness. It was like she no longer had an identity of her own; even my very pointed questions about what she needed to do for herself didn't seem to register. Somehow the conversation always came back to her husband."

When so much of one's life must evolve around another, the boundaries between self and that other person become blurred. Caregiving is a profoundly demanding life event. As the weeks, months, and (in some cases) years go by, it becomes increasingly difficult to separate oneself from the caregiving process.

Yes, we *do* talk more about those we are caring for than of ourselves, and for a very good reason. Their lives and needs absorb us. Our identity and needs become obscured. Our responsibility is to reclaim ourselves.

"What happened was I finally got to the end of my rope." Bea is explaining to the group members what finally made her take some time— long overdue—for herself.

"Spending such long hours at the nursing home, being on an emotional roller coaster for months, not taking very good care of myself, all finally pushed me to the brink. I'm not stupid. I know burnout carries a price tag, sometimes a very high one. It suddenly occurred to me that if I didn't start taking care of myself, my husband wasn't going to have anyone around to take care of him."

Knowing murmurs punctuate Bea's remarks.

"I decided to visit a friend who lives at the coast. I thought it would help to get away for a mini vacation and be with someone who could understand the frustrations I live with day in and day out."

Her words meet with applause.

"But it didn't work out the way I had planned. It turned out that my friend was not about to be dumped on. Every time I started to talk about my husband, she would remind me that everybody has their problems, and she wasn't interested in my complaints about his life, my life, sick beds, nursing homes, and all the rest of it."

A collective groan of outrage goes up from the group.

"No, wait." Bea's hand silences her fellow caregivers. "Let me finish. As much as my friend's words stung, I realized I had a choice. I could either sit around and feel sorry for myself, or I could start enjoying what the weekend *could* be about, other than feeling sorry for myself. And you know what? I made the decision to enjoy myself. And I did! I walked the beach. I watched the waves. I relished the sunsets. Being in nature was the best therapy I could have had. The fact that my friend didn't want to listen to me still hurts, but I think I am the better for it. It forced me to get outside of myself. I came home both relaxed and knowing I won't have to wait so long to get away again."

Bea reclaimed herself. After total emersion in her husband's care, she recognized she had to relinquish her responsibilities temporarily and put her needs first. She had no choice. The emotional and physical stresses of care had reached an alarming degree. Her choice was to take better care of herself or court illness and risk not being able to care for her husband at all.

None of us should wait until we reach the breaking point to begin giving more priority to our needs. Taking time for ourselves is not a luxury; we can't engage in it after the fact. There may not be anything left to take time for.

Burnout comes *after* stress limits have been exceeded. Bea was fortunate. She regrouped with rest and relief from her duties. Had she not taken a long overdue respite break, damage from unrelenting stress could have become irreparable. There are always signals to warn us that stress is extracting too high a toll. Unless we heed these signals and take preventive measures, as did Bea, damage to our health can be in the offing.

THE WARNING SIGNS OF STRESS

- Increased irritability

- Difficulty sleeping, awakening early, or excessive sleeping

- Loss of energy or zest for life

- Becoming increasingly isolated

- Feeling out of control, engaging in uncharacteristic actions or emotions (crying a lot, becoming shrill, focusing on petty things)

- Drinking too many caffeinated beverages or relying too much on nicotine and alcohol, sleeping pills, and other medications

- Changes in the body's normal functioning: a pounding heart, trembling hands, difficulties with digestion

- Becoming forgetful, having problems concentrating

- Becoming less interested in people or activities that were once a source of pleasure

- Eating significantly more or less than usual

- Engaging in compulsive behaviors: constantly cleaning and straightening up or fussing over small, unimportant details

- Becoming accident prone

- Inability to overcome feelings of depression or anxiety

- Denying physical or psychological symptoms: e.g., "There's nothing wrong with taking sleeping pills every night," or "Anybody would be depressed in my situaiton."

- Handling family members less gently or considerately than is customary

- Entertaining suicidal thoughts

While this list is not exhaustive, it does encompass the more common warning signs of stress build-up. In addition, each of us may have our own more specific and unique signs, and, if so, they are the ones to which we must be the most attentive:

"I know when I am reaching my limits," Dorothy reveals. "I become increasingly agitated and edgy. Any little thing sets me off. And if I don't get out and start walking off my nervous agitation, I know for sure I am going to lose my cool."

"What I lose," Sylvia admits, "is my sense of humor. When I get to the point where I can no longer laugh at my problems, I know it's time to put my husband in respite care and get totally away for a week, regardless of what it costs me."

"My voice is my giveaway," Donna joins in. "I talk faster and faster. It's like my words begin to fall over one another: clip, clip, clippity, clip!"

As proficient as most of us are in administering to stress in the family members we care for, we often seem unwilling to take precautions against the escalation of stress in our own lives. To fail to do so because we are unaware of the probable consequences is ignorance but not to do so even when we are aware of the probable consequences is idiocy.

The word "stress" comes from the Latin root word for "strict," meaning narrow or tight. It is an apt derivative. Forces, like caregiving, that limit our freedom of movement are forces that narrow our possibilities for health and wholeness; they tighten and constrict us.

"I'm not stupid," Bea says. "I know burnout comes with a price tag, sometimes a very high price tag."

Bea is not being melodramatic. Stress triggers an inborn response in us which has come to be termed the "fight or flight" reaction. In tense situations, our bodies react by producing adrenalin to increase metabolism, blood pressure, heart rate, rate of breathing, as well as blood flow to muscles. The reaction is a protective one when we are confronted with acute stress. But should the stress remain chronic, the repeated activation of the fight-or-flight response begins to undermine us in subtle but profound ways.

It is not unusual for persons in situations of unrelenting stress to develop blood clots inside the coronary arteries because the arteries remain so constricted. High blood pressure and heart attacks are common stress-related illnesses. The liver can become dysfunctional. Tense muscles can go into chronic spasm. No organ of the body is immune. Even the link between stress and cancer is being explored. Many health problems such as migraine headaches, allergies, and digestive disorders are exacerbated by stress.

The longer the body is mobilized to ward off stress, the more its energy reserves become depleted. As a result, its ability to provide new reserves of energy is seriously impaired. This explains why so many of us who give care are chronically fatigued. With less energy to draw upon, our bodies cannot continue to cope with the drain.

It seems unfair that stress should extract such a toll, especially when its caregiver victims carry out responsibilities that have such a worthwhile purpose. Some people can reduce stress by switching jobs, divesting themselves of primary relationships, making major life style changes. Unfortunately, we do not have such choices. Stress for us will remain an ongoing reality of caregiving. And because it cannot be eliminated, our choices are to undertake to reduce it once it builds and/or to reverse the stress response as it arises.

There are always *two* parts to stress: an *external* side and an *internal* side. The external side consists of the actual stressors themselves. Common caregiver stressors include the physical strains of meeting another's ongoing needs, the inability to structure time for oneself in the face of continuous demands, as well as family frictions and misunderstandings. Seldom do we have any control over the external side of stress.

The internal side of stress has to do with how we *react* to the external stressors. This is the part of stress over which we *can* take control, as seen in the different reactions by two caregivers, both of whom discover bedsores on their family member. One might react with tension and frustration; the other remains more calm, recognizing bedsores to be a hazard of infirmity to be taken in stride. The external stressor is the same, yet the internal reactions are vastly different.

To work with stress at the internal level means learning how to *process* stress differently. It is not possible to stop the fight-or-flight response from occurring when conditions of stress arise. It is possible, however, to deactivate it so that its effects will be less detrimental.

Take Bea, for example, who is on duty at her husband's nursing home. She has already put in a long, exhausting day and is finally prepared to leave when her husband soils himself and his bed clothes. No aides are available to respond to her call. Whatever clean-up will need to be done, Bea will have to do it herself before she can leave if she wants to make certain it gets done within a reasonable amount of time.

As this unexpected stress hits, Bea's anxiety level will automatically climb. Her palms may moisten as her breathing becomes short and shallow. Her muscles will tense; she probably will begin to sweat imperceptibly. Even persons highly skilled in responding to stressful situations will experience the body's automatic fight-or-flight response. But Bea does not need to fight or flee. What she could do is learn to respond to stress in a different way. With practice, she could learn to *deactivate* the stress response before it accelerates into more agitation, more worry, more frustration.

Bea cannot intercept the stress response by willing her heartbeat to slow down, calming her pulse, shutting off her sweat glands, or willfully stopping any of the emotions that may arise in response to her stress: anxiety, worry, anger, frustration. What she *can* do, however, is *reverse* the stress response by altering her breath.

We have at our disposal, in our breathing process, the single most effective way of deactivating the stress response and reversing the fight-or-flight symptoms. When confronted by tense situations that generate stress, slow, deep, mindful breathing is the body's guaranteed way to counter it.

Our breath *is* under our control, even though few of us choose to become conscious of our breathing process. The respiratory center for the body is connected to a large nerve called the *vagus* nerve, which enervates the lungs and heart as well as the chest and abdominal muscles. By regulating our breath, it is possible to slow down to a minimum all physiological activity, including heartbeat. Blood pressure lowers, pulse rate slows, and tense muscles find release as our breathing becomes deep, slow, and conscious.

Emotional states such as anger and fear correspond with shallow, rapid, and irregular breathing. By breathing slowly, deeply, and regularly, tense emotional states subside. Bodies cannot be simultaneously relaxed and anxious. One or the other state will win out. When breath is deep from the diaphragm, our bodies relax, resulting in calmness rather than agitation.

The diaphragm is a large sheet of muscles that extends across the lower edge of the rib cage and attaches to the back. Correct use of the diaphragm is to move it *out* as we inhale, *in* as we exhale. This is precisely the opposite of the way most of us breathe. Most of us breathe from the chest, not the diaphragm. Chest breathing is shallow and less oxygenating. Diaphragm breathing, on the other hand, is deep and allows the lungs to fill more fully, thereby supplying the body with a richer supply of oxygen.

Just as we have been biologically and genetically programmed to respond to stress with the fight-or-flight mechanism, so have we been biologically and genetically programmed to relax. By inhaling and exhaling deeply, from the diaphragm, our muscles release. When muscles release, they relax. Although we breathed this way when we were babies, the response is generally unlearned with the passage of years. With practice, however, it can be relearned.

Doris is a caregiver who has relearned. Because her tension builds throughout the day, she uses a mix of relaxation techniques, among them diaphragm breathing. She does so primarily in the evening to relax tight muscles and calm herself so she can sleep. Using standard guidelines for diaphragm breathing practices, this is what she does:

In a quiet setting, she assumes a comfortable position; usually she is in her nightgown in bed. If she were to be up and dressed, practicing her relaxation response, she would loosen any restrictive clothing. In either case, her eyes would be closed.

She then allows herself to become aware of her breathing, whether she is breathing through her nose or through her mouth.

Next she becomes more aware of her body, taking note of any areas where she may feel tension. She observes the tension but she does not endeavor to change it.

Doris then returns to an awareness of her breathing and begins allowing herself to breathe in deeply and slowly, inhaling through her nose and exhaling through her mouth.

As she exhales, Doris once again becomes aware of her muscles, noticing how they begin to let go. She continues to breathe deeply and evenly, noticing how she feels throughout her body.

Each time she inhales, she makes sure her diaphragm expands and her abdomen pushes out. That way, when she *exhales,* her diaphragm pulls inward. Because this is foreign to how most of us breathe, it is helpful to place a hand on the abdomen to monitor the movements of the diaphragm to make sure diaphragm breathing is being done correctly. Doris continues to breathe in and out *slowly, deeply, evenly.*

She then begins to *inhale* through her nose to the count of one, two, three, four. On the count of "four," she holds her breath for another count of four. Then she *exhales* as slowly and as deeply as she can to the count of one, two, three, four. She repeats this several times, slowly and evenly.

As Doris exhales, she focuses on an awareness of her body, especially her muscles. Sometimes the muscles feel warm; often she feels lighter or tingly. Whatever the bodily sensations, Doris continues to breathe deeply and evenly, enjoying whatever sensations may arise.

Often Doris falls asleep while she is breathing in such a manner.

If she wanted to, she could use the same deep breathing technique during the day in response to stress, or simply to relax.

This way of relaxing is a natural tranquilizer for the nervous system. That is why Doris can fall asleep more easily when doing her deep, relaxing breathing. Unlike tranquilizing drugs that may be effective at first but then lose their power over time, diaphragm breathing is subtle at first but gains in power with repetition and practice. It can be used any time of the day or night when stress threatens or when we need to relax.

Because of our culture's dependence on external agents to relax (drugs, cigarettes, alcohol, food) many people are surprised to discover that something as simple as breath can so alter our body chemistry as well as emotional states. Breath is, however, as complex as it is seemingly simple. In many languages, the word for spirit and breath are the same: in Sanskrit the word for both is *prana,* in Hebrew it is *ruach,* in Greek it is *pneuma,* in Latin it is *spiritus.*

Breath is the very essence of our being. Moreover, its rhythmic movement of cyclic expansion and contraction is both inside our body and without and about it. The same rhythmic pattern of expansion and contraction is found throughout the universe: the alternating cycles of day and night, waking and sleeping, high and low tides, seasonal growth and decay. In a very real sense, it is breath that connects us to the universal rhythms.

Stress-reduction and pain-control programs around the country use breathing as the cornerstone of their treatment programs because it is the most natural way of altering internal physical and emotional states. However, that is not to minimize all the various other ways available to counter stress, many of which are detailed in this book. What is important in stress management is ultimately *less* a particular technique and more the *commitment* to counter stress on a regular and ongoing basis.

The primary reason for stress reduction has to do with our health. If unchecked, stress eventually begins to impair organic function. Silently, insidiously, damage is being done without our even realizing it, until the diseases of stress begin to manifest. Some are psychological and chronic in nature: depression, nervousness, uncontrollable anger. Others are physiological: high blood pressure, chronic muscle tension, ulcers, chronic fatigue syndrome. Caregiving was never meant to exact such a toll. But too often it does.

Why? Are we lazy or too self-indulgent to commit to regular exercise, deep breathing regimes, respite breaks, or the other suggestions discussed in this book or others like it? Certainly not! Anyone who follows us on our rounds for a day and a night will immediately dispel such a myth.

No, the problem is not so much laziness or self-indulgence as it is lack of self-validation. If we are honest about it, there are those among us who do not make the same case for quality care of ourselves that we do for our infirm family member. This is not because we believe ourselves less deserving. *It is because we fail to remember the very reasons we are equally deserving.*

We live in a culture that has become woefully neglectful of the time-honored values of commitment, sacrifice, and the kind of fiercely held compassion that is intolerant of anything less than dignified, quality care. To hold dear such values and to act on them when they are not recognized or reinforced by the world around us does not make them less exemplary. It does mean, though, that validation from others will not be easily attained.

Taking on the care of a frail family member speaks to deeply held moral and ethical values that do set us apart. We have just cause for pride and self-respect, and the right to pamper and celebrate ourselves.

"I took the day off and went with friends to an old-fashioned health resort up in the Columbia Gorge where we could bathe in mineral waters," Sylvia tells the group. "I soaked for forty minutes, then was wrapped in warm blankets and sheets and put to bed where I could rest and doze for as long as I wanted. I don't know when I have ever been so completely relaxed. After we all got up we had a nice lunch and visit in some of the most beautiful surroundings anyone would want to be in. That's not only the kind of day I need, it's the kind of day I *deserve*."

Meeting our needs is not selfish. How could it be? If we are rested, relaxed, and making absolutely certain our needs are met on a regular, ongoing basis, we are more tolerant, less frustrated, are in better humor, and have considerably more of ourselves to give to those who need us.

Enhanced care of family members, however, will always be, in and of itself, insufficient motivation for taking time for ourselves. If enhancing the care we provide is our only motivation for self-care, nurturing ourselves will be sporadic, grudging, and largely ineffective.

We have to respect ourselves enough to see our own lives as worthy of precious care. That is why, individually and in group settings, whenever and wherever possible, it is important to reflect on the qualities that are so right and laudable in ourselves. Lacking validation from the world-at-large, we must do a better job of validating one another: our valor, steadfastness, willingness to give our lives so completely to another human being. There are no better reasons for being found worthy.

"You have to recognize that you *are* worthy," Bea's voice is intense and emphatic as she speaks to the group. "For a long time, although I wasn't about to admit it, I could not put my needs first because I didn't feel worthy, even though I worked long and hard to see that my husband's needs got met. It was like he was entitled to the best of care, but I was not.

"I am not exactly sure what shifted. Something inside you has to change so you know you are worthy; it's hard to explain. Beginning to take respite breaks may have had something to do with it; maybe this group. Anyway, I know now that I actually deserve taking better care of myself. And I just wish I could make all the rest of you feel the same way!"

6

Bea Fyock

Respite Breaks: Nature as a Healing Force

"This is my second marriage, and even though my husband was needing close to twenty-four-hour care when we married, it was a privilege to give it. We had known one another eleven years before we married, and I had never experienced so much affection and attention in all of my adult life. Of course I would take equally good care of him, well or sick.

"I continued to do all of his care for two years. Then it became too taxing for me to keep on so he had to be moved to a foster care home. Later he was transferred to an assisted living center where he has been for the last three years. I go to be with him almost every day.

"The nurses tell me no other resident has family who come so often, stay so long, or do so much. But I have to, both for his sake and for my own. It has been an enormous relief knowing others can give him the physical care I was increasingly unable to give. It also helps knowing how much more social stimulation he receives. The staff really enjoy my husband; they play up to him. He thrives on all their attention. I get a full night's sleep now, which was seldom possible when he was at home.

"I have to say, though, having put him in long-term care has made a lot of things more difficult. There is no comparison in care; I agonize about that and keep thinking there should be a way I could bring him back home. My guilt never goes away. Nor do all the frustrations of trying to oversee and coordinate his care. I know what needs to be done and how to do it, but I am no longer in charge, and I don't enjoy feeling like a top sergeant. Often, the aides are simply not available to do what needs doing.

"Either way, whether you keep a family member at home or have them elsewhere, caregiving is thoroughly draining. Right now, I'm trying to do a better job of taking care of myself. I've finally come to realize that if I get sick, I won't be there at all for him. For the first time in four years I am beginning to take respite breaks. I had my first mini-vacation at the coast and am starting to take one day a week off and not go to the care center at all that day.

"What has helped me to finally start doing a better job of meeting my needs has been the realization that I cannot be totally responsible for my husband's life. True, when we married I gave my life to him in one sense of the word, but I still have to know where that life begins and ends. If I am always taking charge of his life, doing everything for him, protecting him, he is not going to continue to grow in whatever ways are necessary and right for him. Just because a person becomes physically dependent upon others does not mean that that person becomes dependent in every other way. He still has to cultivate the inner resources that will enable him to meet his challenges of living. He still must fight some of his own battles. I can see all this now, but it's taken me awhile to get to such an understanding.

"I do believe everyone has the courage and resolve they need to get through life, but it's up to each person individually to activate those resources. When I was always trying to do for my husband, I was really preventing him from doing what he needed to do for himself. How responsible is that?

"Increasingly I am beginning to understand that my letting go is being fairer to him *and* me. Of course, that is easier to say than do; it's still a push/pull battle for me. I feel so bad on the days I don't go to be with him. Those days I have difficulty living with myself. I have to keep remembering that what I am doing is really for the good of *both* of us.

"Now that I am learning to let go more, my greatest battle is isolation. Your world shrinks so much when you are a caregiver; it shrinks to the size of the world you are stuck in. I used to be a good conversationalist; I have always been a people person and love being around others. But as the months and years go by, and my life is defined almost entirely by caregiving, I find I have less and less to talk about with people.

"My husband doesn't read anymore or watch television. I either don't have the time or am too tired to keep up with current events or engage in the kinds of activities others would find interesting. Unless I am with other caregivers, I stutter and stammer when conversation comes my way. I just can't seem to get into the flow of it anymore. Most of my life I have been happy; now I am emotionally draining to be around. All I seem to be able to talk about are my husband's problems. I hate being like that.

"It helps me to think back to my childhood. My mother was the most wonderful woman; everybody in our town loved her. We grew up during the Depression, and my mother taught us to share everything we had. No matter who came to our door, they were welcome for a meal. My brothers and sisters and I got so used to moving our chairs down the table to make room for others, the gesture was absolutely automatic anytime we were eating and the doorbell rang. Growing up in a family that was so giving and loving I really do believe is the primary reason I am able to find the strength to keep on with my husband's care."

"I am not God," says Bea. "I cannot be totally responsible for my husband's life."

"Taking time for me" became a reality for Bea when she recognized that if she kept putting her husband's needs above her own, there was no way she could take adequate care of herself. And unless she took care of herself, she might not be able to continue caring for her husband. She was also able to understand that if she continued to take more than her share of responsibility for his well-being, she was keeping him from becoming accountable for whatever was necessary for his own continued personal growth.

It is not infrequent in a relationship that one member overfunctions, placing themselves in a "rescue" or "fix-it" position. This is as true for marriages as it is in a parent-child relationship or caregiver-patient relationship. Rather than allowing the other person to manage their own problems, the overfunctioning member takes control. Bea did this, until she realized that she had more pressing responsibilities to herself.

Usually the reason we take on other people's problems to a greater extent than we should is because we are unwilling to put that same energy into solving our own problems. Realizing she was not totally responsible for her husband's well-being was an act of liberation for Bea. She was then able to turn her energy to her *own* needs and begin to do a better job of taking care of herself.

There is nothing wrong with taking responsibility for others. Many caregivers have no choice but to do so. Caring for others is noble and virtuous precisely because one is unselfish enough to invest in the life of another. It is the *excessive* reaction to the concerns of another that is not healthy.

Bea is facing one of the most difficult lessons a caregiver can learn: what *not* to be responsible for; what *not* to take control of. The fact that she is pulling back to allow her husband to struggle with some of his own problems does not mean she has *emotionally* withdrawn from him. Quite the contrary. As she takes better care of her own needs and becomes more rested and relaxed, she will be able to offer more emotional support and interest for whatever difficulties and challenges he needs to face on his own.

Bea took a risk that all caregivers take when they lessen their control over the caregiver situation. Her husband could have become resentful, cantankerous, sullen, uncooperative, or complaining. Fortunately he did not, but some family members do. If caregivers are rested, there is greater likelihood that they will be more patient and more tolerant, and they will have a greater threshold for frustration. Returning from respite to a resentful family member will never be easy, but relaxed caregivers are liable to handle the situation more skillfully than is possible when fatigue and high levels of stress are constant companions.

"Will Bea return to the coast and stay longer?" is not the question to ask. The appropriate question is one that each of us must answer: "*How* and *what* do *we* need to do in order to make renewal and respite ongoing realities in our lives?" What will it take? Strengthened resolve? A willingness to enlist the aid of others? Joining with fellow caregivers who will support our decision? An act of defiance? Asking and taking what we need because no one else will do it for us?

Difficult as the first fledgling steps may be, none of us stand to lose when we take the matter of renewal seriously. If courageous caregivers lose anything it will be tense muscles, nagging frustration, and chronic exhaustion. Some among us, though, may have difficulty deciding what kinds of renewal activities to engage in, it having been so long since we put ourselves first. When that is the case, it may be helpful to reflect on the kinds of activities that once gave us pleasure before life became so constricted by caregiving. To go backward is sometimes to go forward.

Activities that once used to nourish us can do so again if we will permit them. In addition, there are new ones to try. Many of the suggestions in this book are offered in the spirit of exploration. And since they are not a complete inventory by any stretch of the imagination, an awareness of what constitutes renewal for other caregivers may act as a catalyst.

A FEW SUGGESTIONS

- Walking at twilight or early morning
- Sharing a fun experience with a friend
- Playing and visiting with grandchildren
- Playing beloved records or tapes
- Going to (gun, car, home, flower) shows
- Deep breathing for relaxation
- Checking into a bed and breakfast for an overnight
- Meditating with inspirational material
- Building models
- Spending a whole afternoon in the library
- Working with a special craft or hobby
- Going out to eat specifically for the experience of being served
- Dressing up to go some place special
- Watching children in the park
- Taking a very bubbly bubble bath
- Buying a microscope/telescope to get a different view of the world
- Regularly attending a senior center for lunch and recreation
- Taking photographs
- Repotting house plants
- Playing a favorite musical instrument
- Doing absolutely nothing
- Baking something special
- Finishing a project
- Taking a walk in a storm
- Going out on a boat
- Buying new clothes
- Singing with a group
- Watching a sunset
- Joining a club or group activity
- Asking others for hugs
- Taking up bird watching
- Visiting a planetarium
- Writing letters to close friends

Being in nature is an activity that ranks high on Bea's list. When Bea knew she was going to have to take a respite vacation for the sake of her health, there was no doubt in her mind but that it must be to the Oregon coast. She did, of course, have a friend who lived there, someone whom she believed would listen and respond with concern and understanding to her frustrations. There would also be craggy beaches to walk, ocean waves to watch, unimpeded sky and stars, and the timeless cycle of tides.

Although her friend turned out to be unable to give Bea the comfort for which she had hoped, she found it anyway—in Nature. Most of us, likewise, can undoubtedly remember those times when we chose to draw nearer to the natural world and the feelings of release such nearness generated, whether it was walking in the woods, sitting by a waterfall, or wandering on garden pathways.

Perspectives change in Nature. Tomorrow's worries and fears give way to feelings of reassurance. Everything appears in Nature to be as it should be; earth barren or blossoming, trees crooked or straight, flowers in bud or beginning to fade. Decay is natural, necessary, a prelude. Always in nature there is possibility. Crocuses never fail to come up every spring. When life seems tragic and unfair, Nature returns us to promise.

"Ah me," writes an ancient Oriental sage, "I am one who spends his mornings morning glory gazing."

What does a morning glory gazer have in common with Bea walking the beach? Both have come home to the universe. A universe neither would claim to understand, but one they are nonetheless willing to trust as they become quiet and feel more atune with life. Both recognize that the natural world strengthens them and better enables them to meet the challenges at hand.

Most of us who return from encounters with the natural world feel calmer and somehow reassured. Priorities have been reordered as the natural world somehow separates the essentials of life from the nonessentials. That is not all Nature does: Nature relaxes. Nature energizes. Nature heals —in her fields, in her forests, in her splendor, in her peace.

By the FAITH that wildflowers show when they bloom unbidden,
By the CALM of the rivers' flow to a goal that is hidden,
By the STRENGTH of the tree that clings to its deep foundation,
By the COURAGE of birds' light wings on the long migration;
Wonderful spirit of TRUST that abides in nature's breast,
Teach me how to CONFIDE and LIVE my life and REST.

—Henry Van Dyke

Bea experienced that faith, calmness, strength, and courage while at the Oregon coast. And as much as she would like to return there for renewal more often, chances of that happening on a regular basis are as remote for her as they are for most caregivers.

What Bea *can* do is buy herself a pot of chrysanthemums, fill a vase with iris, or plant indoor bulbs to bloom in the darker days ahead. Indoor plants and flowers do not have to be one more thing to take care of. They can be friends and teachers, instructing us in how to CONFIDE . . . TRUST . . . REST. Outside Bea's door, trees, flowers, shrubs, stars, likewise serve as a beacon to the natural world, always so close at hand.

Very small children are adept at beholding the nearby wonders of Nature. What we adults fail to see in a spider's web easily absorbs and enchances a child. A robin's egg, a clump of dandelions, busily scurrying ants making their way along cracks in a driveway, ladybugs perched on laurel leaves are all cause for delight in those who still take the time to see and have the ability to marvel.

Perhaps the most ecstatic experience of Nature must be left to the very young, the nature poets, the morning glory gazers. But for the rest of us, there will always be opportunity for relaxation and healing if we will but turn to Nature for solace. The psalmist did, and his words have never ceased to inspire:

> He maketh me to lie down in green pastures,
> He leadeth me beside the still waters,
> He restoreth my soul.

Comfort is never far from us: in the soaring of sky swallows, in the red glow of the sunset, in the faces of winter pansies undaunted by the snow. Bea found the comfort she sought beside the pounding surf. It was not lasting comfort; Bea did not expect it to be. Again and again she will have to make both the choice and effort for respite and renewal. But next time she may not have to travel so far because she *does* know where to find it: quietly, simply, in nature, where the soul comes to rest.

7

Fighting Self-Pity

"You know one of the things I detest most about caregiving? It's the self-pity. I get in these spaces when I feel so sorry for myself. I know it's selfish. I know it's small. I don't have a fraction of my husband's problems or pain. But there I am anyway, miserable and making sure I keep dwelling on it."

Barbara looks around the group to see if members know what she is talking about. It is clear from their expressions, she speaks for nearly everyone present.

Misery, it is said, loves company. And why shouldn't it? Misery steals over us precisely at those times we are feeling most alone and isolated, physically and emotionally. Lacking the companionship of others who believe in us and urge us on, we court an old reliable friend: self-pity. Ever-lurking in the corners of caregivers' lives, self-pity hooks in as it can, bringing us to despair.

Ready to invade at the slightest provocation, self-pity has its own agenda. It is an agenda of helplessness, one of depression. No wonder Barbara detests her self-pitying states as much as she does.

To some extent, those of us who are caregivers are justified in feeling self-pity. We did not cause the situation for which we are now the caregiver. The stroke happened. The multiple sclerosis evolved. The Lou Gehrig's disease was genetically determined. Yet, whatever the illness or limitation, our lives are in service to it, regardless of how it limits or burdens us.

Self-pity is a feeling. Its spontaneous occurrence in our lives is neither bad nor good. But the powerlessness that underlies self-pity *is* dangerous. To experience self-pity is to feel weak, ineffective, and impotent to act on our own behalf.

Emotions serve the function of messengers in our lives. Self-pity arises in response to the experience of powerlessness. When self-pity is understood in this light, its occurrence can be acknowledged for what it is: a challenge to action.

"I'm a therapist. I'm supposed to know how to handle tough emotional situations. But that doesn't mean I sail right through those of my own all the time. I get in really tight spaces. There is one thing, though, I do know. I'm never as powerless as I think. I may have to seek out help from others: sometimes friends, sometimes professionals. I don't claim to have any kind of formula for not giving in to self-pity. Different strategies work for different people. What is important is never to give up."

Group members do not feel patronized by Lisa's pep talk. She is one of them. It was not until several weeks after joining the group that she revealed to them she was a mental health counselor. They knew her as the wife of a multiple sclerosis victim and the mother of an autistic child; a caregiver doubly in need of support, understanding, and care.

All of us who give care need to hear straight talk about self-pity. We need to know that just because we *feel* powerless to act on our own behalf does not mean we *are* powerless.

Self-pity distorts. When overcome with self-pity it would have us believe that we have less control over our lives than actually is the case. As caregivers we are often in stress. All of us have resolve and resources to draw upon. Self-pity does us grave injustice; we *are not* powerless.

An immediate place to begin is by thinking and communicating in a language of competence rather than one of helplessness. Language is a tool. The way we think and communicate affects how we feel. Feelings of powerlessness intensify when fueled by a language of helplessness.

"If my husband had only seen an attorney and made the proper legal and financial arrangements before he got sick, we wouldn't be in the fix we're in now."

"I just can't help myself; when I'm under stress I eat all the rich food I can get my hands on."

Anytime we believe ourselves to be acted *upon,* we court help-lessness. To feel subject to fate is to be a victim. Self-pity thrives on the vicitm statc. What victims need to know is that seldom does control rest outside of themselves. It may take effort; it may take resolve, but we *can* take control of our lives by being active agents on our own behalf:

"My husband did not see an attorney to make proper legal and finan-cial arrangements before he got sick. We're in a mess, but I'm going to make sure we get the advice we need to straighten out our affairs."

"I can help myself. I will help myself, not to rich foods but to a better understanding of healthier ways to handle stress."

Now control is no longer seen as *external.* The speaker does not feel acted upon, nor is he or she the victim of circumstance. Rather than feel powerless, decisive action is taken. Emphasis is placed on possibility, not helplessness.

Learning to view situations as *challenging* rather than threatening will not come without effort. The natural human reaction to obstacles is generally one of resentment, which manifests as self-pity. Natural as the reaction may be, however, self-pity has a tendency to increase our difficulties as well as being potentially harmful to our psychological and physical health.

If, instead, we can recognize the universality of obstacles in the lives of all people and recognize that in learning to deal with them we are presented with opportunities for inner growth, we put ourselves in the position to fight self-pity rather than become its willing victim.

As long as we remain caregivers, it is probably true that the majority of us will have to keep battling self-pity on a regular and ongoing basis, largely because of the nature of caregiving itself—a draining, isolating, and dcmanding job, intensified by the depletion and discouragement of having to live day in and day out in an atmosphere of sickness and infirmity.

But even though most of us will never win the battle once and for all, through conscious efforts, we can keep from being continually overwhelmed by self-pity. There *are* ways of dealing with obstacles; tried and true ways that have been learned by people who refuse to give in to difficulty without a fight. All of us would do well to employ them on a regular basis.

ACCENTUATE THE POSITIVE

There were two early twentieth-century popularizers of positive think-ing: the minister Norman Vincent Peale and the businessman Dale Carnegie. But not long on their heels, whole schools of psychology followed suit—and with good reason.

Negative thinking and self-pitying put us at risk, physically and psychologically. All of us carry on an internal dialogue. When much of that dialogue is destructive, we become more at risk for heart problems, high blood pressure, and depression.[1]

It is true, of course, that positive thinking when insincerely em-ployed is disgusting in its sticky sweetness. But when sincerely employed, positive thoughts become strong allies in countering self-pity and fostering sound mental health.

"There are lots of things going wrong, but you know, there are a lot of things going right." It is Bea's turn to check in as the group gets under way. "Today I'm not going to tell you about the bad. Instead, let me tell you about the good; it makes me feel better when I do that."

Although they are two opposite ways of evaluating life, negativity and positivity are both *attitudes*. Attitudes, in and of themselves, do not alter conditions in life. Thinking about the good things happening in her life may foster a more positive attitude in Bea, but it will not change the difficulties under which she labors.

Since attitudes are not forces of change, should it then really matter whether we hold a positive or negative outlook on life? *Yes!* As Bea says, thinking positive thoughts makes her *feel* better. Her *attitude* toward life when in a positive frame of reference is significantly different from her attitude when in a negative frame of reference. She sees things as working for her rather than against her.

Feelings follow thoughts. The way we think about something deter-mines how we feel about it. By focusing on the positive aspects of her life, Bea generates feelings of well-being. Emotionaly she *does* feel better than when negativity holds sway, with its resultant feelings of self-pity and depression.

COUNT YOUR BLESSINGS

A great many philosophers and most of the great religious traditions advise: think on the things that are good, beautiful, and true. We are given the moment. We have not made it. We have not bought it. We may not even like it one bit. But if we receive it creatively, there is always within the moment an opportunity to find something worthwhile.

"There are times when I don't want to go on living," Eileen says haltingly. "But I make myself think of my grandson. What a beautiful and sensitive child he is. How close we are with him not having a mother living with him. He is a gift life has given me. When I think about him, I know I am not going to let the burdens of caregiving defeat me."

No one cay say what effort it may take for Eileen to focus on the blessing of her grandson. Doing so does not come easily in lives where maintaining some semblance of equanimity is an ongoing battle. Many of us will have to struggle like Eileen, particularly when the depleting aspects of caregiving make us prime candidates for self-pity. But whatever effort we do make is certain to be worth it, for whenever gratitude is expressed, despair has a way of making itself more scarce.

REORIENTING THOUGHTS

Abraham Lincoln had his own way of phrasing this principle: "A man is about as happy as he makes up his mind to be." Making up our minds to be happy is often a matter of substitution; replacing thoughts of worry, self-pity, and negativity, with more pleasant satisfying ones.

"I lay awake in bed at night and make my head remember the beautiful scenic areas where my husband and I loved to camp. It's the best way I have of relaxing so I can unwind and get to sleep. Otherwise I am a great one for staying awake worrying and feeling sorry for myself. My favorite place to go in my mind's eye is to the Canadian Rockies. The last time we were there I sat for two or three hours impressing the view into my mind. I must have known we would not be returning. But as it is, I can now go back there any time in my head and instantly relax."

   Doris smiles as she speaks, as though a part of her right now is back in the Rockies.

Doris consciously chooses thoughts that work to her benefit. She has learned that happy memories allow her to relax. She needs her sleep. The morning will bring its share of cares and worries. Purposefully she makes use of her imagination to return to places and times of joy. She could as easily move forward in her imagination in anticipation of happy times: specialties of family festivities; respite vacations; and upcoming programs, visits, and celebrations all offer possibilities for reorientation of thoughts. Whether looking forward, backward, or squarely in the present, we *are* about as happy as we make up our minds to be.

PRAYER

Surrender is a more humble approach to letting go of self-pity. Surrender acknowledges that we are unable to help ourselves or accomplish what needs to be done in and of our own accord.

Those of us with a religious orientation who struggle daily to overcome the ways in which we limit ourselves only to meet with more failure than success, need to be reminded to seek beyond ourselves. Surrender is a giving over. The concept seems simple, but it is not. Surrender takes unfathomable resolve. Moreover, yielding our will is no guarantee that we will always find the comfort we seek.

"I think it's great that some of you find that God usually comes to your rescue when you pray for help," Barbara tells the group. "But that is not always my experience. And I don't know why. Sometimes I say: 'God, I haven't moved, so where are you?' But there is no answer."

Those who always find their God available upon request are among the minority. Barbara's experience is the more common. It takes considerable trust to make an act of surrender; all the more so when often it seems as though supplication meets with no discernable result. Yet, such is the very nature of faith. That is why nurturing faith and yielding self-pity to prayer necessitates constant reminders: for examples, inspirational readings, prayer groups, and formal worship services. Combined with *effort* on the part of the faithful, however, we must always acknowledge the role of Grace in life, without which perfect surrender is largely impossible.

ASK QUESTIONS DESIGNED TO EVOKE SOLUTIONS

- "How can I enjoy what the day is about in addition to its worries and its cares?"

- "How can I stop my head from worrying about finances for the remainder of the morning?"

- "What do I have to do to stop resenting my family member right now?"

This technique does not attempt in any way to deny difficult situations. It acknowledges their full reality in order to do something more productive about them than worry or become immersed in self-pity.

Although the questions need to be asked in seriousness, their answers can be visualized playfully. The four-year-old, in the imaginative recesses of our mind will respond very differently from the serious forty-year-old or the wise eighty-year-old. There are many voices to be heard within all of us. Rather than listening to the voice we think we "should" heed, we would do well to listen to the voice we find most appealing.

As sound as the above suggestions are, they may not come easily in practice. Changing behaviors is never easy. This is even more true during times of stress and strain when we are drained of much of the energy needed to make the effort to change.

Even so, we *are* responsible for ourselves. Self-pity makes us fugitives from ourselves, placing blame for our feelings on others and on circumstances; forcing us to feel more powerless than we really are. Although self-pity may not be entirely conquerable, it can be kept more manageable if we are willing to confront it every chance we get.

It is important to recognize that self-pitying thoughts, like worry and other forms of negativity, have insufferable tenacity. Banishing them at will is usually futile. Thoughts that we try to push out of our minds return with intensity because strain and effort exert a counterforce of their own, strengthening the thoughts rather than weakening them.

A more useful approach is to enlist the powers of imagination. Self-pitying thoughts and other negative feelings are more readily dispelled by using a creative approach. When such thoughts threaten, we would do well to visualize a red flag or a large red stop sign. Heed its message: S T O P!

"What's going to happen to me if . . . S T O P!
"I'm not going to get through this . . . S T O P!
"Nobody understands what I am . . . S T O P!

Visualization is an extremely powerful tool. It is sometimes referred to as "the key to the gods." If a red flag or a stop sign are not dramatic enough to get results, a more arresting visual image can be used. We can see ourselves at the batter's mound, slamming the self-pitying thoughts out of the stadium. Any kind of image can be used: a strong original one of our own making will be the best.

The object is to *stop the unproductive thoughts.* Once that has been accomplished, we can then substitute positive thoughts, count our blessings, reorient our thinking, or use the most helpful mix of the suggestions given above.

Still, there will be those times when even effort and resolve meet with minimal success. These are the times when we need support and strength from others. Comfort, consolation, and the urging of family and friends are often integral to our being able to continue on helping ourselves. Most of us need encouragement in difficult undertakings. We need to know there is a cheering section behind us.

When efforts to help ourselves fail, it may not be because we who engage in them have failed. It may be that we are failed by the very persons who could help us succeed.

"I can't live in a vacuum," Doris explains to the group by way of **introduction at the first session she attends. "I can do a lot on my own to help myself, and I do. But I also know when to admit that I need support. That's why I am here. I have to be with others who understand what I am going through. I have to be with people who reach out to one another."**

Psychological sophistication has conferred upon us the ability to advise on all manner and form of life's challenges. We are the better for it. But if we have to go it all alone, only the most stalwart will meet with success. The way is too rocky. The way is too rough. Like Doris, most of us cannot live in a vacuum.

Support and encouragement are energizing forces. Teams do better on their home courts because of local fan applause. Caregivers are no different. We, too, need the good wishes and kind words of others to do our best.

We also need to be around those who are dealing with difficulties just as we are. Placing ourselves in situations where we are able to offer needed compassion and care is one of the most effective ways of moving beyond self-pity. We need something bigger than our own pain if we are going to be able to grow beyond it.

"This sounds terrible to say," concedes Marie, "but I don't feel nearly as sorry for myself when I leave here, knowing what others of you are going through."

What a difference it makes when people draw near to support one another. Suddenly we are able to remember what we otherwise come so close to forgetting: yes, we *can* triumph, sometimes in small ways, sometimes in big ones. We are not as bad off as we thought. We just needed steadying hands to help us regain our balance . . . and our resolve.

"I got so tired of feeling trashed; one day off a week wasn't really doing it," Bea tells her friends. "Our doctor could see that I was going downhill and needed a real vacation but that I wasn't going to do anything about it. Bless his heart, you know what he did? He told my husband he was sending me away for a couple of weeks. He said I had been working very hard and needed a vacation so I didn't become his patient, too. My husband went right along with the idea. After all, it was 'doctor's orders!' My attitude changed overnight!" Bea pauses to laugh before she details the plans for her first long vacation in seven years.

"Give us the name and number of your doctor," group members chorus.

NOTE

1. Joseph Martorano and John P. Kildahl, *Beyond Negative Thinking: Breaking the Cycle of Depression and Negative Thought* (New York: Plenum Press, 1989).

8

Lisa Lieberman

Caring for the Caregivers

"Some months ago, I went on a raft trip for three days with eleven other women. The trip marked a turning point for me. Up until then, I had adapted to living at the edge of limits, getting through each day as it came, but not having enough energy left over to do an adequate job of meeting my own needs.

"My husband was diagnosed with multiple sclerosis in 1982. The deterioration has been gradual. He gets around in a motorized cart and is still able to manage most of his personal needs. Much of my time and energy goes into the care of our son, who is autistic. One of the reasons I had not taken time off for a respite vacation was my fear that our son would have another seizure while I was gone.

"Fortunately, a friend of mine recognized how much I needed a break. All the arrangements for the trip had been made; I didn't have to do any of the planning for it. My job was to pack my bags, hire someone who could take over for me at home, and go. I pulled through on all three!

"The first day out, I worried the whole time. It wasn't until the second day of the trip that I started to relax and enjoy myself. But when I was finally able to, the old me broke through. I was more surprised than my friends. I played. I sang. I laughed. I returned home feeling like a new person.

"I will always be grateful to my friend for inviting me to go. Initiating a trip like that would have been impossible for me. When you are a caregiver and your life must constantly revolve around others' needs, your own get pushed aside. You know you should do a better job of taking care of yourself, but there are always priorities that get in the way. With my child and husband disabled, I am constantly faced with obligations and responsibilities that force my needs to take a back seat, often by necessity. But there are those times when my needs rightfully should come first. I'm getting much better at letting them do so. It's a lot easier, though, with some support. That's why I'm so indebted to my friend for the rafting trip.

"When friends or family step in without being asked and do thoughtful things for me, it's like being given a new lease on life. Simple gestures are often the most touching: for example, going out to dinner with friends and having one of them take the initiative to push my husband's wheelchair in from the parking lot, up the ramp, and into the dining room.

"Of course I like the grand acts of thoughtfulness, too: those of friends who put a lot of energy into helping meet some very special needs. When we lived in Yakima, we had friends who, every summer, came with their horse to take us hiking. A horse was the only way my husband could go on such a trip. They would put him on the horse each day so he could hike and climb right along with us. They never waited for us to ask; they knew how special it was for us and proceeded to do it.

"Caregivers not only need that kind of thoughtfulness, we deserve it. By profession I am a therapist. My specialty is families who live with disability and infirmity. In many ways, my preparation began in childhood with disability in my own family. Because I grew up having to help others, counseling was a natural choice. Between my clinical practice and a lifetime of caregiving experience, I know a lot about coping. But I also know the best of coping skills eventually break down for most of us unless they are supplemented with support from others.

"I can give just so much myself. Beyond that point, I start to lose it. The strength and initiative I need to work on my family's behalf, much less mine, just aren't there. Yet the minute others offer to help, I start regrouping. Energy and enthusiasm start flowing right back, and I can do what needs to be done. It was that way with the horse trip and the rafting vacation. Once others got the ball rolling, I could wholeheartedly join in.

"People who genuinely want to understand what I am going through also mean a lot to me. I don't have much use for advice givers. And I don't let the fix-it-uppers waste my time. But give me those people who want to hear my story, and I open my heart to them. Some friends have told me that they hesitate to express themselves about our situation because they think it will be too painful for me to hear their feelings of sorrow, helplessness, and anguish. Others think it is too painful for me to talk about what I have to deal with. They are all wrong. I need to know people sincerely care enough about me to listen. I need to know people want to understand what life is like for us.

"One of the reasons I believe I am able to be an effective therapist for people who live with disability is that I genuinely want to understand what they are going through. We become companions on a journey together. I'm the one with the compass because of my training and long experience. But the real reason the journey is satisfying is that we are taking it together in the spirit of understanding and compassion.

"My husband works in the field of cellular communication systems for disabled populations. He finds similar phenomena: his own special needs have made him far more sensitive to those of the people he helps.

"What bothers me the most about working in the field of disability is the insensitivity of people. Behaviors can be so inappropriate and hurtful. I want to shake people and tell them they 'should' know better. Some should. But I am convinced that most just don't know any better. And I am also convinced that our job as caregivers is to educate people about what we do and don't need.

"Recently I have been trying to do more of that myself. I have started to give workshops and lectures in the community to help raise people's awareness about what families with special needs go through. It really seems to help. I'm convinced that people will do better if we show them how.

"In the months ahead, I also plan to get back to my music and a regular exercise program. Exercise in the past played a big role in keeping my stress level manageable and my energy level up. With exercise and my support systems in place, I think I can do everything that needs to be done without neglecting myself in the process. Finding skilled, loving people to help care for our son has been an enormous help. I now have more time for work and myself.

A little while back, I joined a neighborhood bunko-game group. I never would have thought I was the bunko type, but that kind of activity meets needs that can't get met in other ways. I look forward to those evenings, especially their rowdy laughter. I don't think about my caregiving responsibilities or the concerns of my clients. I just relax for two hours and enjoy being a regular member of the human race."

A person whose caregiving is on both a personal and a professional level cannot help but attract the admiration of others. Few of us would envy Lisa or want to trade places with her. Some will label her a glutton for punishment, while others will contend that she is of the "super-woman" breed.

Neither is correct. Like most caregivers, Lisa struggles to bring balance to her life. At this point in time, she has her support systems in place. She is more strongly committed to taking the time she needs for herself. She is able to let others know how their actions affect her, both positively and negatively. She does not claim to have fully mastered the formula for caregiver health and well-being. Realist that Lisa is, she knows that mastery is not possible, but it gives her a goal to strive toward.

Increasingly Lisa is advocating for fellow caregivers in a larger public forum. In community groups, in lectures, in classes, and in workshops, her message is singular and to the point: this is what caregiving is about; here is how you can help us.

Lisa knows firsthand that caregivers are an at-risk population. But for her, finding fault serves no productive purpose. Her own needs did not get met by complaining, hanging back, or hoping for change. Change, according to Lisa, happens when we make it happen. She recognizes that insensitivity often emerges from ignorance. As a caregiver advocate she intends to change that.

There is no time to lose. Demographics are changing. In a few short years, family caregiving will become the norm, not the exception. Our nation's elderly population is growing faster than any other age group. With projected health-care costs likewise growing at an alarming rate, home care will be the one affordable option for families with fragile elders and/or disabled members. And while most will not want or need rafting trips or excursions to the mountains, all will need the kind of thoughtfulness and support those actions represent.

Lisa suspects that that kind of support will not happen unless we who are the caregivers help make it happen. She's right.

Unfortunately, helping those around us to become more sensitive to our needs is not an easy task. Many of us who give care have difficulty asserting ourselves. It is easier for Lisa. She is younger, better educated, and more confident of her message and mission than the majority of those in her situation. But then, hers is the circuit of lecture halls and public forums. Our outreach need not be so formidable. It can begin much more simply with our own family and friends and anyone else whose life touches ours. Many of them will listen, if we have the courage to speak from our hearts. Knowing where to start may be the most difficult obstacle. We tend to hold so much inside.

An edict may be the place to begin. Edicts give cause for thought and stir us to action. They can be photocopied, posted, mailed, and used to pace discussion with family and friends. We may find we do not have to suffer in silence if we take the initiative to break that silence.

THE CAREGIVERS' EDICT

DON'T ASK US TO LET YOU KNOW WHAT YOU CAN DO FOR US. TAKE THE INITIATIVE AND DO WHAT YOU SENSE NEEDS TO BE DONE.

Even though your offer may be sincere, we find it hard to ask for what we need:

- When our energy and strength are often so low that we feel diminished, having to ask someone for what we need makes us feel even smaller. As it is, we struggle to maintain an adequate self-image. Often we fail. Don't wait for us to ask. You may wait forever.

- We fear rejection. Our world has narrowed dramatically from what it once was. With sickness as our primary focus, we are less enjoyable to be around. People are uncomfortable around chronic illness and disability. We hesitate to call friends; we doubt if they really want to remain a part of our lives.

- We are used to giving, not taking. We feel awkward about being on the receiving end. If we take, we feel we should be able to reciprocate. We canot do so easily. So much of our time and energy goes into caregiving that thinking how we can give back adds to our stress.

- Often we are so overwhelmed with everything we would like to have done for us that we don't know where to begin asking. And even if we do, getting the courage to act may be difficult.

- We have a lot of pride, though some of it may be false pride. But self-esteem suffers when you are a caregiver. Confidence and competence shrink except for those tasks and responsibilities that accompany caregiving. Pride may be the one component of self-esteem that we still have. Let us hold on to it.

- When people say to us "Let me know if I can help you," it is often their way of placing responsibility elsewhere and thereby avoiding it. Other times it is said in such a perfunctory, insincere manner, we don't even take the gesture at face value.

ON THE OTHER HAND

- We *do* recognize that a general offer of help can be sincere, and it is made because people honestly do not know what would be helpful. When that is the case, those who make the offer should explain their frustrations and work with us to come up with useful suggestions.

ASK HOW WE ARE DOING

- We know the family members for whom we are caring need as much attention and concern as they can be given. *But so do we.* We get exhausted by always being on the giving end. We need to be the recipients of attention and concern ourselves. Often those we attend to can no longer respond to our needs. Unless we put back what we put out, we risk being less than we want to be, both for the family member to whom we give care, and for ourselves.

- We relax and unburden when others genuinely want to know how things are with us. But here is a useful pointer: When you ask how we are doing, be prepared to accept our feelings even if they are disturbing ones. Anger and resentment are common emotions for caregivers. We are not bad people because we experience them. If telling you how we feel makes you uncomfortable, tell us. Please do not change the subject, make a joke, or talk about somebody you know to be worse off.

DO NOT TELL US HOW COURAGEOUS WE ARE
OR HOW YOU ENVY OUR STRENGTH

- You do not see us when we are overcome with despair or guilt-ridden for having become angry, irritable, or petty with those to whom we provide care. Nor do you see how exhausted we become from trying to be strong and courageous. If you did, you would understand why we want to be weak and cared for once in awhile.

- If you put us up on a pedestal where we do not belong, we will just be more isolated. If you persist in seeing us as strong and courageous, we can't share our vulnerabilities, even though to do so would be a great help.

- Tell us our eyes are sky blue. Tell us we've got the long tapered fingers of a writer. Tell us we would make a circus clown laugh through his tears. Tell us anything but that we are strong and courageous.

DON'T GIVE ADVICE OR TRY TO FIX OUR LIVES

- If the problems we face could be fixed, we would have fixed them by now. We have probably tried more strategies than you ever thought existed! We know advice is often well meaning, but giving advice is like saying, "I know the answer, why don't you?" It is not advice that we need.

- A lot of our problems are simply not solvable. Please remember that. Substitute understanding and compassion for moralizing and pushing *your* agenda for *our* lives.

HELP US SHARE OUR FEELINGS—
YOU WILL COME TO KNOW US BETTER

- If we can share our feelings, you will better understand our humanness. We recognize that you may not want to be around us if we talk too openly about feeling scared, lonely, or depressed. On the other hand, being given the opportunity to share those feelings could bring us closer.

- We need to be able to drop our defenses and feel more relaxed. Sharing feelings helps us to do that. It also helps to know that others genuinely care enough to want to listen.

FORCE LEISURE ON US

- Bring us a movie pass or a ticket to a concert. Help us make all the arrangements so when we leave we can shut the door behind us without looking back. Some of us will protest when you make your offer, but don't take no for an answer:

      * When your life is about giving, it is hard to let go and let someone look after your interests.

      * We forget how much good it does when we get away from our responsibilities. Staying home may not be fun, but it may be more secure than breaking out of our routine.

      * Some of us need companionship in order to reap the benefits of getting away. Don't just send us away; come with us.

HELP US PLAY

- Life is such serious business when you are a caregiver. It's easy to forget how to have fun. We need opportunities to smile and laugh and enjoy ourselves: a comical or inspirational movie, a children's theater performance, an evening of cards, a rousing pro basketball game, an excursion on a steamboat.

- Brainstorm with us about opportunities for play, then make certain we don't miss out on them. We do need to talk out problems on occasion, but we also need opportunities to enjoy ourselves so much that we forget about our cares.

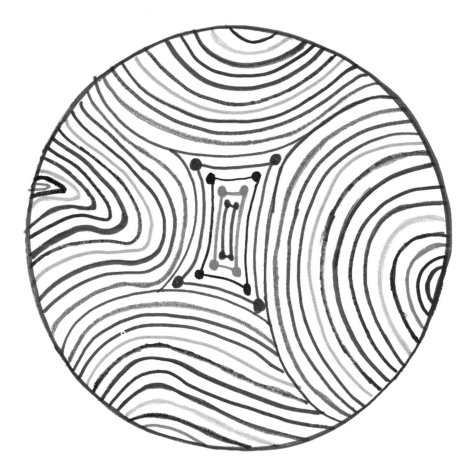

9

Of Moles, Dead Ends,
and Other Creative Adventures

"This is a mole, buried deep in the ground. This is a rock blocking his entry way. He has no way to surface. He can't get light. He can't get air. He can't get help."

Holding up her drawing, Barbara points to the mole, the rock, the tunnel. Group members have been depicting in a series of three drawings how they are currently feeling, how they would *prefer* to be feeling, and how to change from the one to the other.

Pointing to the second frame of her drawing, Barbara shows the rock pushed away from the hole.

"If the rock can just get out of the way, I will be able to surface. To me, that means getting out from under it all, a chance to rest and unwind from the tension. A chance to breathe!"

Heads nod. The caregivers know all about blockages and rocks. A picture *is* worth a thousand words.

Caregiving trials and tribulations will never disappear on command. Rocks are rocks. Holes are holes. We worry a lot about our trials and tribulations, often unaware that worry itself saps vitality and erodes self-confidence. The caregivers gathered are hoping to worry less about their problems by learning a more creative use of their imaginations. Rocks need to be kept in perspective.

Helplessness is not meant to triumph over possibility—particularly for caregivers.

For us, helplessness translates into less than effective care for a family member and less than effective care for ourselves. None of us can afford that kind of helplessness.

Moles are not helpless creatures. Barbara chose her animal wisely. Moles are tenacious. They find ways to surface, no matter how rocky the terrain.

How might Barbara get from a blocked hole to an unblocked one? Her third frame holds the clue; a large balloon is in the process of being popped with a pin.

Barbara tells the group that the balloon represents the martyr part of herself; the part that tries to be all things to all people at the expense of her own emotional and physical health. Her mole gets buried when she persists in taking on more than she can realistically handle.

The drawing reveals what Barbara needs to do on her own behalf: lessen the reins, learn to say no, and put herself first, at least some of the time.

Her friends give Barbara encouragement for doing what she knows she needs to do. She is not certain she can. Habits are years in the making. Talking about it does help; Barbara laughs at her martyrdom, moles, and balloons, and relaxes.

Such an activity gives group members instruction in working imaginatively on their own behalf. Most of us do not put our imaginations to work very often for our own benefit.

Of course, our imaginations work overtime when we worry. Worry is the *negative* use of the imagination. When we worry, we make mental pictures in our heads of worst-case scenarios. We imagine what is going to happen IF . . . The more vivid and ruminating our imagination, the more we become distressed. We worry all the more. The pattern becomes circular and self-defeating as our stress intensifies.

Creative thinking is the *constructive* use of the imagination. Creative thinking breaks the pattern of worry. By picturing in our mind's eye how we can change our situation, we take the emphasis off defeat and place it on possibility.

Group exercises that use art to show how to work creatively with imagination are not intimidating when participants recognize that artistic ability is not the point. The point is self-help, sprinkled liberally with laughter.

Sylvia holds up her drawing. Laughter drowns out her explanation. A picture of a woman with one finger plugged into an electrical outlet fills the first frame. Every hair on the woman's head sticks up

corkscrew fashion. Her dress, her face, her neck, her fingers, her toes are stiff with electrical charge. She is totally wired!

"Oh, you do know how we feel," members of the group chortle.

We who give care need to laugh, play, and create in order to balance the more serious times when our responsibilities weigh heavily. Activities that accomplish that purpose are not frivolous. They are life sustaining. It is a measure of sound mental health to be able to look squarely at the frustrations that plague us and poke fun at them. To be able to laugh about a situation may well keep us from being defeated by it.

Sylvia's wired woman is not going to have the last say. Sylvia may not be able to totally unplug, but as long as she can laugh, she retains control, even though all circuits hit overload.

Realistically, though, there will be times when overloaded circuits get jammed; when even laughter cannot break through.

A car, speeding almost out of control, moves through the third frame of a group member's drawing. Getting in her car and escaping, she tells the group, is the only way she can see to break free of the stress under which she labors. Her drawing is cause for sadness and concern; it mirrors such hopelessness. Problem solving, even creative problem solving, is not so easy to do when we need to cut and run.

Futility is a feeling we caregivers know well. Most of the time the feeling comes and it goes. But should the feeling become unrelenting, our health is placed at risk.

It is unfortunate in this group member's estimation that there appear no creative choices in her dilemma. What the drawing does provide, however, is an outlet for her feelings. Had her frustrations continued to remain bottled up, she would be even more drained of coping energies.

Art, in all its expressive forms, is often produced out of anger, frustration, or an intense need to communicate. *It is particularly under stress that energy levels build.* Along with the build-up comes a deep inner need for expressions. Giving the energy creative vent is often the most productive and safest way of providing an outlet.

Any creative act—drawing, handiwork, gardening, sculpting, whatever—will help release pent-up feelings, which, if not given expression in some *positive* fashion, have a way of lashing back.

Many of the behaviors of which we caregivers are not proud come about as a result of frustrated energies suddenly erupting. We snap, argue, sneer, and blow up. Our frustrations are discharged, but in ways that we regret.

Making sure we have outlets for our frustrations is an integral part of "taking time for me." Wielding knitting needles, kneading the bread dough, hooking a rug, or hammering nails, are much more than simple hobbies. They are a way to stay sane.

"Okay, so it's not exactly what you'd call a piece of art, but it gets out how I feel." Lisa holds up her picture. Jagged lines of color spew out in a frenzy.

"Today it seems I have been on the run since I got out of bed. Dashing here. Dashing there. These lines say it all. I needed those crayons!"

A glowing candle fills Lisa's third frame.

"My place of inner peace. That's what the candle represents. In the early morning hours I can sit quietly, meditatively, I know I can handle whatever a day holds. To do so, though, I have to take the time to come back to myself, starting from a place of calm integration rather than in a track runner's stance."

The afternoon of art is a worthwhile use of the Portland caregivers' time. That does not mean others of us need to rush out to buy crayons and drawing paper. Any type of creative project can have similar results, provided we find it enjoyable.

Our grandmothers and great-grandmothers quilted, knitted, and crocheted their way out and around a good deal of life's stresses and strains. Moreover, they had worthwhile accomplishments to show for their efforts: needed housewares and clothing along with calmer emotional states.

Brain waves change both in amplitude and frequency during the times we engage ourselves creatively. Creative work—e.g., the quiet focusing on hobbies—generates a brain-wave pattern known as the *alpha* wave, a slower, more relaxed electrical pulsing of energy. Alpha states are cultivated by people who meditate and engage in biofeedback for purposes of stress reduction. These brain waves are more restful and therapeutic for the body than the *beta* brain-wave pattern, which characterizes active thinking and verbal interaction.

The generation of alpha waves during the creative act explains why the *process* of creating is more important than the end result. Don has many more hours to put in before his model ship is complete. He is in no great hurry. The positive feelings he experiences during his hours spent building are more important to him; that will be his sense of accomplishment when the boat is finished. Helen is not up at midnight baking because she wants others to exclaim over her wares in the morning. She simply has no intention of lying in bed worrying when it feels so much better to cream butter and shape cookies.

It is not by chance that members of the caregiver group enjoy themselves when they have opportunity to work creatively and constructively with their stressors. And it is a far better use of their time than sitting together sharing miseries, and staying identified with their infirm family members' problems.

Creative problem solving does not ignore problem states. It gives credence to them *in order to change them.*

We need to share our burdens and to talk about our family members with understanding friends and relatives. Likewise, in a group setting, sharing stories of personal pain can be a healing experience when listeners are sympathetic and supportive.

Personal stories of pain, however, *can* become narcissistic, obsessional, and a safe way to pass time without having to take the necessary steps and risks to introduce change. There is an enormous difference between becoming engulfed in worry over one's problems and working creatively to transform them.

It is yet another afternoon of creativity for the Portland caregiver group. Members sit fashioning play dough into shapes and designs reflecting current frustrations. They then go on to sculpt ideas to help them consider possible solutions.

Michelle contorts her chunk into knots and intricate twists mirroring her tense emotional state. The sculpting allows her to release a sufficient amount of tension so that she can reflect on the curative forces in her life in a more relaxed way.

As it comes Michelle's time to share, she first holds up her twisted lump: "No doubt you can guess how I feel," she gives a brittle laugh. "It's the same deadening routine day after day. I take care of my husband's needs. In return, I can't do anything right in his eyes. He gets angry. He closes off and won't talk. On top of that, I can't get away. Our apartment is tiny. There is no place I can go and shut the door, except to the bathroom. That's where I go to cry."

There is quiet in the room. Michelle's pain becomes everyone's pain.

"But . . .," there is a pause as Michelle picks up the three cunningly shaped figures she has sculpted: one female, two males. "These

are my two sons and daughter. They all live out of state. I haven't wanted to let them know what's happening to their father and how tough things have been getting for me. But I think I am going to change that. They all care a lot about us and would support me in any way. I know that. Just talking with them more often and being real honest would be a big help right now. I think I can bear up if I can get understanding and backing."

Opportunity for creative expression serves Michelle well. She releases frustration and moves on to problem solving. What the afternoon does not change, however, is the "deadening sameness" to her days.

Deadening sameness is a perennial caregiver plague. Many of our acts are repetitious; our routines are fixed. Many of our chores are performed automatically with little room for invention. Deadening sameness goes with the job.

Fortunately, there is a way to counter the monotony. Get out in the garden: pull weeds, plant seeds, prune suckers. Buy a paint-by-number kit. Forget that art teachers don't like them. They are an excellent way to relax. Embroider a drab piece of clothing. Build toys for the underprivileged. Create something. Create *anything*. But keep on creating. Break the monotony of housekeeping chores and nursing routines.

Creative work *energizes*. Creative work *renews*. By allowing us to stretch and beckon out the unused parts of ourselves, creative activity lets us become much more than the sum total of our caregiving acts. Deadening sameness is tolerable when it is not the whole of life, but only one part of it.

And yet . . . given the choice of picking up an embroidery needle or crying in the bathroom, some of us are still going to be found in the bathroom. Not because we are lazy, immersed in self-pity, or don't agree that creative projects can be as enjoyable as they are necessary for health.

When stress levels are exceedingly high, the thought of acting on our own behalf in unfamiliar ways can be an unlikely possibility. We may first need encouragement and support to pick up our crayons, *if* we can get it.

Marie points to her first drawing. It is a steep, narrow road angling downward, ending in an embankment of mud. Flanking the road are a series of signs reading: BEWARE! STEEP DOWN HILL! ONE WAY! DEAD END!

Adjacent to the road and mud bank in Marie's second frame is a glowing sun. She wants to be creative, life-giving, radiant. How can she better navigate the treacherous road so as to get to the sun?

"COME JOIN MY CLUB," reads a long sign-up list in Marie's third frame. There are slots for twenty signatures of those who will lend support and help. Marie knows precarious journeys aren't meant to be undertaken alone. And she is willing to ask for what she needs.

Chapters on creativity merit satisfactory endings. This chapter does not have one. Marie's drawing gets passed around, but no one makes the gesture of signing it. Either her friends do not take her artistic request seriously or they know not to sign because to do so would be a hollow gesture.

By and large, members' own personal struggles appear to preempt outreach to one another any time other than during formal meeting times. None of them are likely to commit to what they cannot or will not follow up on.

The ideal for Marie, of course, would be to have members of her caregiver support group be in close communication with her in between sessions. That does not appear possible, even though she has made an attempt to ask for it. The group simply does not operate in this capacity. Outside of meetings, Marie has no real depth of contact with group members. Even telephone calls are the exception, not the rule. As is usually the case in our fast-moving, stressful world, people are so involved in their own struggles, they find it difficult to set aside the time to reach out to others in between more formal times of fellowship.

Perhaps in the years to come there will be a restructuring of society such that, as in earlier times in our country, communities of support will again become the norm, not the exception. Let us hope it will not take siege or suffering to weld us into such communities.

The support group movement appears to be among the social forces now at work steering us away from the alienating lifestyles that have kept us removed from one another. And although it is our weaknesses that are enabling us to find one another again, in the future, it will be our strengths.

Because the support group movement is still very much in its infancy, Marie's caregiver support group does not yet have a model for meeting the support needs of one another beyond actual sessions. This is true likewise of many other support groups, whether they are organized around Twelve Step issues, AIDS issues, job-finding issues, the scores of the needs that bring people closer together. But as the group movement matures, support may be recognized as having less to do with clock time or scheduled meeting dates and more to do with the willingness to bond deeply in our shared humanity when and as need arises.

None of this is consolation for Marie. Her need for support and help is immediate. There seems little likelihood that either will be met. This is a chapter that cannot close with more advice on caregiver renewal. This is a chapter that closes with pathos.

10

Marie Goodwin

Dealing with Guilt:
"To Everything There Is a Season . . ."

"Crazy silly lady. That's the description that has always fit me. I may be one stressed caregiver, but there's a part of me that is always going to keep on dancing anyway.

"My singing group is rehearsing its Christmas program. I am going to dance in it as well as sing. The songs are the cheerful and merry Christmas songs; the choreography is upbeat. I have always sung in groups of some kind or another, usually church choirs. This kind of program, though, is where I have the most fun because it really lets me kick up my heels. I also play bridge and go regularly to an exercise class. For the first few years of full-time caregiving, I dropped away from all activities, but finally came back to them to stay sane.

"Even so, I feel like two different people. The public me is much like my old self: independent, fun to be with, sensitive to others' needs, sometimes pretty outrageous. But I'm not that way at home. At home, I am increasingly on edge. I lose my cool too much. I am tense and worried. It's getting more and more difficult to be calm and accepting of my husband's compulsions, his touchiness, his agitation.

"Two weeks ago, I left him in a local respite care center and went to visit my daughter and her family in Cleveland for two weeks. It was so relaxing to get away and to be the one who was spoiled for a change! You would think being away from caregiving for two whole weeks would have given me a new lease on life, or at least the patience to do a better job handling my responsibilities. It didn't. Almost the moment I walked back into the house, I felt irritable. That is why I know I have to make major changes. It is getting more and more difficult for me to take care of my husband at home. I cannot keep on being two different people. I want to be crazy silly Marie, not Marie going crazy.

"Twelve years ago my husband was diagnosed with Parkinson's disease. The first six years we were able to keep reasonably active, doing most of the things we had planned for our retirement. Then as the disease progressed, our life became more and more curtailed. Complicating my husband's Parkinson's are severe anxiety attacks; he is almost always tense and worried. We moved to Portland to be near our son as the condition worsened, and I became a full-time caregiver.

"My family, friends, and neighbors have all tried to give me advice. Some years ago they told me I had to start taking better care of myself. They encouraged me to take up some of the activities I had given up. I knew they were right, but I couldn't bring myself to do so. Guilt was a big part of it. I didn't feel right about being the one to go out and have a good time when my husband couldn't. Besides, I didn't think it was safe to leave him alone.

"But as much as I couldn't let myself break away, I knew deep down I would be able to break away when the time was somehow right. And one day the time was right. That was the day it suddenly dawned on me: if my husband was going to fall, he was going to fall whether I was there or not. I also realized that if I left him alone, I was giving him the satisfaction of being able to do something on his own, looking after himself the best he could while I was gone. That reevaluation of our situation made it suddenly okay to start doing the things I once used to do. When the timing was right, all the obstacles keeping me from making changes fell away.

"I have the feeling that the same thing is going to happen when the time comes to put my husband in long-term care. For some time now, family and friends have been urging me to take that step. Two years ago neurologists told me they had patients far less advanced than my husband who were already in nursing home care. But the time was not yet right for me to do so, and it is still not right. What is starting to happen, though, is that I am beginning to evaluate our situation differently.

"I never used to worry about getting sick. Now I do. I worry a lot. I know people can live in high-stress situations just so long before they get sick. I know that not being able to keep from being irritable is a signal that I'm on overload. All the positive things I do for myself away from home, the things that used to help relieve stress, aren't so useful anymore.

"My family and my support group are helping me to reevaluate my feelings. It has always seemed selfish to put my needs before my husband's, especially since he has been sick. But others are helping me realize that it is also selfish not to be the kind of grandmother that my grandchildren need. As long as I have to be involved with my husband's care, I can see them only very infrequently. I want to be a real grandma, not an absentee one. I'm also recognizing that it is selfish if I damage my health in the process of caregiving. Then I will become a burden on *our* children. They already have one sick parent; they don't need two.

"Guilt is the biggest obstacle keeping me from placing my husband in long term care. Duty and obligation are my middle names. I come from Dutch/German stock. I am stubborn and tenacious. I don't like giving up. But I don't like to be tense, irritable, and resentful either. When my husband sees me like that, it adds to his agitation and worries. In many ways it seems fairer for us to make a change in living arrangements. I know professional health-care workers would be calmer with him and better able to handle his agitation. He is a lot more confused now. When he came home from the respite care center after I got back from my vacation, it took him a while to recognize where he was.

"Funny thing. I always wanted to be a nurse, but I never completed my nurse's training. Well, I have been a dedicated nurse for some years now. But I think it is a different kind of nursing I need to get into—like helping other caregivers. I have a lot of compassion and my experiences and knowledge of resources have proved valuable to other caregivers. I want to do more of that kind of outreach, and I know I will. First, though, I have to act on the decision to no longer care for my husband at home. Making that change will be the hardest thing I have had to do in all my married life. Like I said, guilt is a big obstacle, but there is something more as well. Deep down I know the timing is not exactly right. I don't know when it will be. I just know I will recognize it when it is."

An enormous change looms ahead for Marie, one of the most drastic and dramatic she has had to face in her forty-nine years of marriage. Years of caregiving have taken their toll: Marie is tired, and her health is increasingly at risk. Tension and irritability are too often her companions. Ahead lies the agony caregivers face when they recognize they can no longer continue as primary caregivers and must place their loved one in institutional care.

For years, Marie has fought such a change, even though neurologists, family, and friends have urged her to do so. She still is not ready, even though she recognizes that such a change is in the offing. For now, however, two impediments stand in the way: guilt and timing.

Anytime we think or act in a way that goes against our values, guilt arises. As Marie says, she comes from German/Dutch stock, an ethnic culture whose members were taught at a young age to weather adversity. Both her religious upbringing and sex-role conditioning taught her to place doing unto others over doing for herself. It is only natural, then, that she feels guilt at the thought of institutionalizing her husband. She thinks if she could overcome these feelings, the changes ahead might be easier. The reality is, few of us who give care ever gain total mastery over this complex emotion.

Guilt is often referred to as a "camouflage" emotion because it is often used to mask other feelings that create considerable anxiety if we allow them into awareness. Whether we would admit it or not, many of us find it less disturbing to feel guilt than the emotions of anger or selfishness. When this is the case, we use guilt to camouflage either or both emotions, much as Marie has.

Of all people, caregivers are not "supposed" to be selfish. Women, in particular, have been conditioned by society to believe it is selfish to place their own needs above those of others. Men who are caregivers frequently feel the same way. For a long period of time Marie did not join groups, take classes, or go on vacations by herself to visit her children because to do so made her feel guilty, i.e., she was *unselfishly* thinking only of her needs.

With long-term-care placement looming in the future, it is only to be expected that Marie would again experience guilt, as would any of us. With some knowledge of what institutionalization is like, it seems to her that she is sacrificing her husband's comfort and well-being to satisfy her own. The harsh verdict of selfishness, however, is frequently self-imposed.

Fortunately, Marie is beginning to be more objective about those feelings, and with the help of family and friends she is reevaluating them. In the long run may it not be *more* selfish to remain her husband's primary caregiver? Certainly that will be true if escalating stress causes her to become ill, thus creating another burden on her children. Also, by not being an active and involved grandmother with grandchildren, isn't Marie selfishly denying the children her love and attention? Although she very much wants to be involved in their lives, her care responsibilities do not permit it.

The more objective Marie can continue to become, the better able she will be to take constructive action to meet *her* needs as well as her husband's. Institutionalization is never easy. Action does not need to be taken soon, but only when Marie is able to put her feelings in the proper perspective.

When anger underlies the guilt, the situation changes. We who give care often think we "should" not be angry with a family member who is sick, incapacitated, and needful. Often we try to pretend that our anger does not exist. But it does, and we know it. When that happens, we end up feeling guilty for being angry.

In reality, we who give care have a right to be angry. Caregiving puts grave restrictions on our lives. There are the never-ending demands that control us in atmospheres of sickness. We become increasingly isolated; few of us have access to the support that would make our job more manageable.

It is not wrong to feel anger under such circumstances. The emotion is an entirely legitimate one. How we *express* the anger is what will determine whether it is unproductive for us. And it is difficult to express anger in a *productive* fashion. Most of us become irritable and defensive when we are angry. Often we say or do things for which we are later sorry. There are many books and guidelines available offering suggestions for expressing anger appropriately. They are all insightful to read, but difficult to implement in actual practice. Like all emotions anger is irrational: we rarely become calm and collected enough to make rational and deliberate decisions about how to express the feeling.

Rather than focus on how to express anger productively, the more useful question to ask is *why* the anger is surfacing. In a very general way, it can be said that a certain amount of caregiver anger arises because *our* own needs are being neglected. If we can do a better job of identifying what those needs are and making certain they get met as much as possible, we are apt to find a dramatic reduction in irritability and anger.

Most of us do not take sufficient time to relax and nurture ourselves. We get used up. The more bankrupt we become, the greater the potential for angry explosions or deep-seated guilt feelings which mask the anger.

Some years ago, in order to be a full-time caregiver, Marie dropped out of activities that she found fulfilling. After a period of time, however, she was able to overcome her guilt feelings about participating in outside activities without her husband. She recognized that she had to do a better job of meeting her own needs. As she did so, she became less irritable and tense.

Taking time for herself and finding stimulation and enjoyment outside of the home changed Marie's attitude and stress level for the better; caregiving became a manageable responsibility rather than a resented one. Recently, though, her irritability has returned in spite of continuing with several satisfying activities. Now, however, the reason for Marie's irritability is different. Her husband's need for care is escalating. As much as she does not want to admit it, she is reaching the limits of her endurance. Anger and irritability are forcing her to look at the fact that she needs to allow others who are more trained than she to take over her husband's primary care.

Although Marie knows what lies behind her current frustration and what she must do about it, she still harbors guilt connected with nursing home placement. Most all of us would also. *Guilt is a normal response for any of us to feel under the circumstances, and we cannot rid ourselves of it easily or permanently.* What can be helpful, however, is to recognize when parts of guilt are associated with unrealistic expectations. That we *can* do something about it, just as we can begin to control aspects of guilt we use to camouflage our feelings of anger and selfishness.

Part of loving another person is wanting to save them from as much pain and suffering as we can. That is why most of us do not want to place our family member in long-term care. But, we also have to distinguish between what we *can* and *cannot* do. There are wants and desires we are powerless to do anything about.

In spite of her husband's deteriorating mental state and more arduous care demands, Marie, by her own admission, is stubborn and tenacious. She does not like to give up, even when her personal expectations exceed her capabilities. But the reality is that Marie has done as much as she can do for as long as she has been able. *Family, friends, and professionals need to commend her for continuing with the stresses of caregiving for as long as she has before reaching the limits of her endurance.* If more of us received this kind of validation for our caregiving, we would feel less guilty about not doing "enough."

Anytime we have to go against deeply held values and beliefs, guilt arises. The very thought of institutionalization goes against the values and beliefs of many caregivers. We want those we love to be cared for with dignity and compassion, particularly as death nears. We know impersonal care is less likely to be dignified, compassionate care. What is more important to guard against, however, is intensifying guilt by agonizing about those situations *over which we have no control.*

Marie does not want to place her husband in a facility that does not meet her standards. But no facility is likely to meet them; no form of impersonal care can. Institutional care will never approximate good family care. It is not that most long-term-care personnel are uncaring, but it must be recognized that paid care is seldom devoted care. The interest and affection of health-care workers can be entirely genuine, but when the work day is over, they return to their own homes. Their skill, training, and concern are for their patients; their devotion will remain to their own families.

It would be more helpful for Marie to acknowledge that fact and concentrate on making the best long-term-placement decision she can, weighing the factors that must be taken into consideration when selecting a facility. Beyond that, she has little control, *except:*

(1) to take action if the facility turns out in any way to be neglectful of her husband's physical or emotional health;

(2) to *oversee* and *supplement* the care her husband is given;

(3) and to ensure that her husband is given the personalized care and the dignity, respect, and compassion to which he is entitled.

If the care center she selects does not educate or empower her to function in these capacities, then she must educate and empower herself with materials that will show her how to do so.*

Those of us who are plagued by strong guilt feelings need to follow Marie's lead and share them with family and friends. Situations that cause us to feel guilt often change as we are helped to evaluate them from a different perspective. Subjective doubts can be countered by reality checks from others. In this manner, we are able to become more realistic and objective about the caregiving situation.

Among all the stresses caregivers face, emotional strains are now recognized to be the most severe.[1] Guilt, anger, depression, helplessness, anxiety, and lowered morale are far more disruptive to our lives than the physically demanding care for which we are responsible. For

---

*See Katherine Karr, *Promises to Keep: The Family's Role in Nursing Home Care.* Prometheus Books, Buffalo, New York, 1991.

health reasons it is critically important to work through these problem emotions when they strike.

The most *ineffective* way of dealing with emotions is solitude. By ourselves it is difficult to break free of guilt, anger, depression, loneliness, and frustration in ways that are productive and healthy. Left to our own devices, we tend to find temporary often unsatisfactory relief from these problem emotions: food, drugs, or sleep. In the company of others, however, we are more apt to talk out, sort through, and reevaluate our feelings; in so doing we can more healthfully discharge such emotions. Being able to see our feelings in a different light we gain the power to transform them.

Nevertheless, trying to get a *permanent* hold on problem emotions will not be possible for most of us. Caregiving is fraught with ambiguity and paradox. On the one hand, taking care of an infirm family member is fulfilling, growth producing, and ennobling. On the other, it is enormously stressful and can be tragically painful. Having to live with such paradox is, of itself, unnerving. Some days we are grateful and feel privileged to be caregivers. Other days we are filled with frustration and anger. We go to bed exhausted, not knowing how we can cope with another day; yet we get up, find ways of renewing our resolve, and continue on.

Given the ongoing tensions of caregiving, whatever form it may take, we need to learn to be gentle with ourselves. Confronting suffering on a daily basis has a way of making even the most stalwart among us petty and small on occasion. Our job is a hard one; it comes with occupational hazards; disruptive emotions that *will* get the better of us. Guilt, anger, selfishness, and frustration are all normal, understandable feelings in our circumstances. We need to feel compassion for ourselves rather than recrimination when we cannot ease our emotional pain.

Compassion, concern, and loyalty all characterize Marie's long years of caregiving. Those years are not coming to a close. They are changing in degree and kind. The time nears for which Marie has been waiting:

> To everything there is a season;
> A time for every purpose under heaven . . .
> A time to weep and a time to laugh,
> A time to mourn and a time to dance . . .

Cycles are the foundational pattern of time; Nature's guarantee that there is a season for everything. Seasons are a part of human cycles of existence as they are of Nature. There is a time for waiting, a time for acting, a time for putting another's needs first, and a time for giving priority to taking care of ourselves.

Marie will not hurry time. Nor will she ignore the signs indicating that changes are coming. Like all of us, she is human, fallible, and not easily distanced from strong emotional energies. But beneath the guilt and irritability lies a deeper intuitive awareness. Marie knows there will be a "right" time to make the necessary changes in caregiving, whether guilt is present or not. She waits for that time with trust.

Guilt, futility, and worry are *fear based;* not so with trust. Trust is born of faith and wisdom. Marie's long years of living have confirmed for her that there is a patterning to life. Guilt-ridden though she may be, deep in her heart Marie knows she is not giving up, nor resigning herself to be less than she wants to be. She is, instead, relinquishing to a wisdom of cycles and seasons and mysteries not for us to understand, but rather for us to marvel at and honor.

"This, too, will pass," seers have said. Summer splendor gives way to the decay of autumn leaves. Winter's bleakness closes in, then the earth breaks into spring blossom. And so Marie waits for seasons of caregiving to change. Will it be a time for weeping or a time for laughing; a time for mourning or a time for dancing? Marie does not know. In guilt she agonizes. In trust, she waits.

NOTE

1. Brody, "Parent Care as a Normative Family Stress."

11

Playing Away Cares

**"I would like to have more fun and be more fun to have around,"
Bea shares with her friends. "The problem is, I don't know how to
have fun anymore. I haven't played in so long that if someone were
to ask me what I wanted to do, I wouldn't even know what to answer.
What I do know is that if someone else got things going, I would
join right in!"**

Caregiving of infirm family members is serious business. It is not just
Bea who has forgotten how to play; many of us have. The heaviness
of our responsibilities weighs us down. A form of grimness often
accompanies the care of the sick and dying. Our worries and our cares
keep us from opening wide our arms of life until we, too, forget what
it is like to play at all.

Can we become again as little children? There are such good reasons for doing so: Play is freeing. Play is energizing. Play is fun. Play
is therapeutic. Play is delighting in the world. Play is a fitting counter-
balance for work and worries. It is not repressive to play. It is life-
giving.

Small children need no excuse to play. Whether they are hob-
nobbing with neighboring cats, making secret forays into flower gardens,
fashioning mud bricks and sand castles, dressing up, or arming for
knight battles, children spontaneously reach out in play to embrace
their world.

The need to embrace the world in play is never outgrown. However,
it does get buried under adult responsibilities and cares, and once buried,
it can be difficult to revive and release. Like Bea, we may need others
to get us started.

"I'm going to throw this pillow at someone." Twirling a plush golden pillow, Sylvia gives a mock throw, then continues. "And whoever gets it has to tell us where they were born and some highlights of their life. Then that person will toss the pillow along to someone else until we have all had a chance to share." After we've discovered who we are in addition to caregivers, our reward will be game time!

Sylvia holds up papers with lists of scrambled words: reabotof oottlffs nboes eleh soopttef ote nlia oels.

"The first person to unscramble all these foot words gets to be my demonstration model while I pair everyone up and show you how to give the best foot massages that will relax every pore in your body!"

Well into overtime, group members are still sprawled out on couches and chairs, laughing, talking, massaging. No one is making a move to go home. Nor do their demeanors bear much resemblance to the tense men and women who walked into the room two hours earlier.

The afternoon of pillow-tossing, word game, and massage serves its purpose. By instigating a spirit of play, Sylvia beckons forth vitalizing forces of renewal in her friends, allowing play to do what play does best: replace tension with the uplifting energies created by laughter and pure delight.

Energy fields charged with joy force tensions to relax their hold. It is impossible to be tense and relaxed simultaneously. Of course, the caregivers were in no hurry to take leave of their afternoon of play, which enabled them to relax and for at least two hours, put their cares on the run.

True, no problems had been solved. None of the caregivers present were permanently absolved of the stresses they faced on the home front. The afternoon was pure escapism. But as all of us know who give care, "escapes" are often our salvation. What we need more of are escapes that are not fattening, passive, or addictive. And in the world of healthy escapes, very little can beat the allure of play.

The first to respond to the "play" problem-solving question, Bea licks her lips and begins: "The first thing I would do with caregivers who do not know how to play is take them out for old fashioned milk shakes, the kind that are so thick you have to eat them with a spoon!"

Small groups have broken off from the larger group to playfully brainstorm what to do with caregivers who have forgotten how to play.

"Pinochle! I haven't played it in years," Barbara exclaims. "I loved pinochle. That's a great game to break people out."

"How about volleyball?" Sylvia joins in. "I'm a great server! Smacking balls beats breaking dishes when you've got to have something to throw!"

"Water is so playful cascading down fountains," Bea observes. "We could go on a fountain walking tour. Kids will be spashing; maybe we'll kick off our shoes and go join in!"

"And why not rent a van while we're at it," Barbara is not to be outdone. "We can go anywhere we want . . . to the beach, up to Victoria (British Columbia), go to the wax museum, the Buchart Gardens, stay at the Empress. If we run out of money, we can come home and camp on our four acres. Better yet, why not move into a condominium together and play every day!"

Barbara's suggestion meets with applause from Sylvia.

"You're on! Then the next time my husband says he is moving out, I'll say, 'No you're not. I'm the one who is moving!'"

Merriment rules as playful ideas keep flowing.

"You know what I think?" says Bea. "I think it is wonderful to laugh like this."

Sparking ideas for play opens the door to fun and laughter. By becoming partners in play, Bea, Sylvia, and Barbara create their own special and endearing form of communication. The imaginary wish list may or may not be forgotten in the days to come as the three become immersed in their caregiving tasks. But what will linger is the reciprocal delight experienced when imagination is given playful reign. For a part of the afternoon, they stand outside of time, creating a world of their own, as do children: a world of laughter and joy, a world of their very own fashioning, one of uplifting energies that vitalize while forging close bonds between them.

Caregiving so contracts our world that many of us have difficulty thinking or talking about anything other than our caregiver situation. We *need* play. We need it to liberate us and broaden our world.

Play does not ask of us to be something we are not: well read, erudite, socially engaged, politically astute. All that play asks is that we exercise imagination. And when we do, whether for thick milk shakes, traveling vans, or cascading fountains, we find meaningful communication no longer eludes us. Quite the contrary. Playful interaction allows us to be the engaging conversationalists we didn't know we could be.

Throw the dice. Move the pegs. Take a card from the pile. Answer true.

- **What piece of advice would you give to a young man about to be married?**

- **How would you change the world to make it a better place to live if you had enough power?**

- **Thinking back, what can you identify as a beneficial turning point in your life?**

- **If you could be invisible, where would you go? What part in a parade would you like to be?**

Seated around a table playing the UNGAME,* caregivers at play are once again far removed from their caregiving frustrations. There is laughter. There is wit. There is eager anticipation. There is perceptive repose. Self-pity and frustrations are dislodged by play. Worlds expand as caregivers stretch to be more than they remembered they could be.

It is yet another afternoon of play for the Portland caregivers. Not pinochle but a board game changes what could have been a morose afternoon into a convivial gathering. Gripes do not seem to need much of an airing when caregivers are challenged to be more than the sum total of their limitations. For while limitations are an inescapable part of caregiving, there is more to caregiving than its limitations.

Too many of us tend to get stuck like record player needles in the limiting parts of our lives. Play moves us beyond those limits. Play shakes us loose, and upside down. The weight drops out of our pockets.

Regardless of the constrictions under which we labor, there is still a richness of life to be had for the asking. Play helps us to push out restrictive boundaries. Children continually use play to do this. The bravado of pirate swagger allows a shy child to be forward. Swinging boldly on the monkey bars the sheltered child begins to take risks. Little girls draw their guns and, giving strident battlefield commands, acquaint themselves with assertive forms of power.

"What part of the parade do I want to be? Well, that's not so hard to answer." Eileen pauses only briefly.

"In the band, of course! I would be the young lady right in the front. The one with the baton, you know; twirling it smartly, throwing it skyward until it touches the clouds, stepping high, stepping proud!"

---

*The UNGAME is a popular board game devised by a counselor to help enhance communication between people.

Inside a caregiver who is beleaguered by tension and stress prances a little drum majorette. Calling up her image delights Eileen. She giggles and sits up straighter. Her cheeks flush; her dark eyes sparkle.

"The next time things get out of hand," Eileen laughs, "maybe instead of throwing up my hands, I'll go out in the backyard and start throwing my baton!"

Playfully, Eileen acknowledges she *can* challenge frustration. By activating a healthier sense of her self imaginatively through play, Eileen is no longer the diminished caregiver who walked into the afternoon session. Moreover, the drum majorette can stage a return, nudging Eileen's elbow when stress escalates and self-pity threatens. Whether or not she *will* return is up to Eileen. But at least play has helped broaden Eileen's sense of herself, providing her with creative ways to work on her own behalf if she so chooses.

We caregivers are *not* victims. Self-pity would perhaps like to have us think so, but what does self-pity know? Its knowledge base is too restricted. In reality, we have a whole cast of characters ready to come forth when we put out the call.

Children know there is a whole cast of characters within. They play at being astronauts, nurses, ferocious animals, rock stars, aliens, race car drivers. They let their imagination teach them about possibility. They do not say, "I am only a child. I cannot be this or that." They say, "Through the powers of my imagination I can experience being whoever and whatever I want to be in a way that helps me understand and make my way in the world."

Why shouldn't adults play at being childlike? Why shouldn't Eileen play at being a drum majorette, especially during those very times that the twirl of a baton may mean the difference between a smile and a scream? We need all the help we can get, and help is as close as the blink of an eye.

There is always an inner festival going on; it has to do with the life of our creative spirit. Sometimes it may take the form of a baton twirler, sometimes the cowardly lion of Oz who has learned to roar back, sometimes an army of storm troopers ready to march us out of the sick room to a big screen comedy at a motion theater complex.

Playful use of the imagination puts us in contact with the greater potentials of our lives. A certain amount of the frustration and confusion many of us experience may well have less to do with our actual caregiving situation and more to do with having pushed down the ability to play imaginatively in our heads. To recapture that ability may be to find we have more friends, allies, and redeemers than we ever dreamed possible. There *is* a big parade going on inside of us. Beat the drums; wave the flags; let imagination soar.

And if we cannot? Then we must ask some hard questions about where we stand with control.

Control is an expression of power, although not the most mature expression. Control has a need to be right at all costs. It needs to ensure that life goes according to prearranged scripts. Control makes us attempt to do things that may be quite unnecessary in the larger scheme of life. Control keeps us from lightening up and being candidates for play.

"Health-care workers tell me I'm not taking control of the situation," a caregiver confides. "I diaper my husband at night so I don't have to get up several times to toilet him. Now that he has begun pulling the diapers off, I just let him lie on the urine soaked pads. The health-care workers object. They see my actions as selfish. I see them as survival. Mine and his. I am not pleasant to be around when I am exhausted from lack of sleep."

This chapter is about play. There is nothing playful about this caregiver's story, save this: She is not being stoical. She is not attempting to be rigid and controlling. She is not attempting to do everything "right." She can let go, more so than those of us who overdeveloped the habit of unselfishness to remain tightly in control. And it is the willingness to let go that makes the opening for play to come into our lives.

Couldn't more of us, likewise, spend less time trying to do everything "right" and instead learn to spend time twirling batons? Our playful side has a more relaxed attitude toward what is "right" and what is "wrong" than does our controlling side. Play is not black or white, nor is it rigid. Play experiments with possibility. Play takes risks and, in so doing, stumbles upon undreamed of possibilities.

Any hairshirts we wear are of our own making, and they merit replacement. Life may not be fun or fair right now. But for those of us who are determined, there is always *some* playful way to conspire with drum majorettes.

"I've joined a hiking group that meets on the same day as this caregivers' group, so I won't be seeing you except on stormy, wet days," Dorothy reveals to the caregivers assembled. I know it helps to come here and share common frustrations, but do you know what helps me even more? A day to forget them while I thoroughly enjoy myself!"

12

Sylvia Wilson

The Importance of Humor

"Can you believe me, at sixty-eight, taking a job as a waitress? I'd never done anything like that before, but I just had to get out of the house and be with people. Friends of mine got me the job. It was at a Thai neighborhood restaurant for two hours every Saturday night. I looked forward to it all week. I could get out of the house, leave my husband in front of the T.V., break the monotony and stress of our life, and earn money besides! I've always liked serving people in some way. The customers were nice; so were the owners. I'd still be there today if they hadn't gone out of business.

"I'd like to keep on waitressing; I just don't know who's going to hire a seventy-year-old woman to wait tables. But it won't hurt to look around. There's a new adult day care center opening not far from here where I can place my husband. That way I can be gone for longer periods of time.

"People tell me I should get involved with volunteer work. I tell them that since my husband's stroke ten years ago, I have been doing volunteer work: hard work, day in and day out. It's the kind of volunteer work no one thanks you for. If I can get away, I want to get paid for what I do. Earning money makes me feel worthwhile.

"After my husband's stroke, the neurologists at the hospital told me to place him in a nursing home. They said he would be too difficult to take care of because of the kind of brain damage he had. They were right about the brain damage. His belligerence, negativity, agitation, memory loss, inability to relate to me, and his constant panic attacks made the first two years a nightmare. I couldn't have gotten through them if I didn't have my faith. I had to keep saying over and over, 'I can't do it God. You're going to have to because I'm going to fall flat on my face.' I never have fallen flat on my face. The strength has always been there, somehow. I keep asking, and I keep receiving. I pray that will always be the case.

"I don't mean to sound like I always carry it off. I have days when I get angry and days when I get discouraged. So far I haven't let them get the best of me, because I know the way I handle myself is a reflection of my faith.

"The doctors didn't think my husband would get any better, but he has. Being at home rather than institutionalized has made the difference. That's the positive side. The down side is that he will always be horribly difficult to be around. The belligerence and negativity have not changed and they never will. He does not know I am his wife; no matter how many times I tell him. His memory is permanently impaired. Everything I tell him is immediately forgotten.

"My patience is tried every single day of my life. Before my husband got sick, I used to pray for patience; now I'm in a situation where I have no choice *but* to exercise patience. Goes to show, you have to be careful what you ask for. You'll get it. Life is that way. We get what we need, just not on our terms! The blessing in all this is that I have a sense of humor.

"Laughter has always come easy for me. I can see the funny side of things, no matter how rough they get, and I love to pun. The problem is, you can't laugh by yourself. There are good comedy programs on television but it's not the same as laughing together with others. It doesn't feel as good. There's no laughter in this house anymore, and that's partly why it gets so depressing.

"One of the reasons I joined the caregivers group was to be able to laugh. When we are sitting around taking turns talking about how difficult things are in our lives, I can see people getting anxious, knowing their turn is coming, and it will be painful to talk. So I say something funny to break up the anxiety. It helps my friends and it helps me.

"What would help us a lot more is to go out and socialize together. I don't want to sit around and talk about problems all the time; I face them at home. I want to get out and have some fun. But it's hard to ask for what you need. I get so much rejection: people no longer come to visit; neighbors stop being neighborly; people tell me to call them and let them know what they can do to be of help, but none of them take the initiative to call me.

"A therapist once came to our group and said it was wrong to think we were weak if we asked for help. He said strong people can ask for help because they are able to recognize what they need. He made it sound easy. It's not. I am able to ask God to meet my needs. That's easier than asking human beings. But you need help from both ends.

"When those rare people do reach out, without having to be asked, it makes you feel like a million dollars. Last year my church group somehow found out when my birthday was and had a party for me with cake and a gift. I felt so special. They couldn't believe it when I told them it was my seventieth birthday. They wanted to know how I managed to keep looking so young. 'Well,' I told them, 'they say it's all in your genes, and I must have designer jeans!'"

Sylvia has a funny bone, and she may well have been born with it. But for those of us who weren't, humor doesn't have to elude us. As much as we need the Sylvias, we also need to cultivate a sense of humor in ourselves.

Humor is an *attitude,* a state of mind, a way of placing in perspective the events life hands us. Philosophers have pointed out that comedy and tragedy are but two different ways of looking at the same event.

Stress is seldom caused by an external event. It is our *perception* of the event that creates the problem. Barbara came to one meeting, exhausted from being up most of the night adjusting her husband's medication. She told friends she finally got to bed at dawn, only to be kept awake by the birds who made what to her was an unbearable racket. As much as she hated to admit it, all she could think about was going out and shooting every bird in sight. Sylvia told her next time to do it, but not every bird, just the crows. Barbara began laughing and became visibly relaxed.

A humorous interpretation of an unsettling event can go a long way in breaking its hold on us. The next time Barbara finds herself in the same situation, she may remember Sylvia's humor and refuse to let the birds be such an intrusion on her sleep.

Laughter can take negatives and turn them into positives. When we can joke about a tough situation, we are really saying: "I know this is serious. But I *am* in control. I *am* in command of the situation."

When we have burdens, most of us tend to overfocus on them. Laughter breaks the tendency to obsess, bringing in the freshness of an enlarged viewpoint. With a change in perspective, it is easier to detach from difficulties. Situations that otherwise threaten to defeat us become instead, with laughter, occasions for triumph.

Interpersonal problems also have a way of yielding in the face of laughter. The shortest distance between two persons may well be a smile; when we smile and laugh, we relax. The more relaxed we are, the less apt we are to be argumentative and defensive.

As caregivers, we would do well to draw on this property of laughter as often as possible, particularly if infirm family members resent and resist being told what to do, even when it is in their best interest. Playful directives rather than autocratic ones will be much more apt to generate cooperation.

It doesn't take a quick wit to be humorous, maybe just a playful spirit. St. Theresa, an early mystic of the Catholic Church, was riding one day in a bumpy horse-drawn cart during a torrential rainstorm. The cart hit a pothole, throwing Theresa head-first into the mud. At that moment she was certain she heard the voice of Jesus speak to her from the heavens: "This is how I treat my friends, Theresa." Wiping the mud from her face, she is reputed to have shot back: "No wonder you have so few of them!"

The playful little child inside all of us may not surface as easily as it did for St. Theresa, but that is no excuse to keep it under wraps. Most of us, too early and too harshly, have repressed our playful side, sacrificing its gaiety for the serious concerns of adulthood. These same concerns threaten to overwhelm us unless our playful side can provide a needed balance.

One way to bring out this spirit of play is in the company of those who enjoy laughter on a regular basis. As much as caregivers need understanding and supportive relationships, we also need friendships where laughter flows easily and freely. Whether we join a caregiver support group, an exercise class, a church club, or an interest group may be less important than whether members are fun to be around and laughter is a welcome friend.

Sylvia is one who finds it easier to laugh in the company of others than by herself. And although that is true for most of us, the times when we are unable to do so need not be sad, serious times—at least not if our playful side recognizes the importance of creating a climate of laughter. Situation comedies fill the television airwaves. Most libraries have collections of humorous literature: joke books number in the hundreds, and situational comics from well-known cartoonists are collected in anthologies. Jokes and cartoons that make us laugh can be clipped and saved, even placed around the house in areas where we need reminders to smile.

The noted writer Norman Cousins created an atmosphere of laughter around himself, which in many people's eyes healed him of a life-threatening disease. He later went on to write about his experiences in the best-seller book *Anatomy of an Illness.*[1]

Returning from a physically draining trip abroad, Mr. Cousins came down with a fever that rapidly progressed into a serious illness requiring hospital care. Tests determined that he was suffering from a rare collagen disease. Collagen binds connective tissue and is essential in holding the cells and structures of the body together. Mr. Cousins was told that his prospects for recovery were dim; his joints continued their deterioration.

Refusing to accept this diagnosis, Mr. Cousins proceeded to take charge of his own treatment. He had read about the adverse consequence of negative emotions on the body and reasoned that if these emotions had in any way predisposed him to the illness, positive emotions might be able to restore balance and help him recover.

Obtaining funny movies and old Candid Camera segments, he had them shown in his hospital room. One ten-minute period of laughter yielded two hours of painless sleep in his otherwise never-ending bout with pain. More remarkable, hospital measures of inflammation before and after each session of laughter verified the cumulative improvement directly attributed to his positive attitude.

As the hospital stay lengthened into months, Mr. Cousins decided that institutional food was not sufficiently nutritious for him. Because he was also concerned about his laughter bothering other patients, and did not want technicians drawing his blood so often, Mr. Cousins checked himself out of the hospital and into a hotel room where he could continue with his laughter therapy. Improvement steadily continued, and ten years later when he wrote his book, he had recovered, despite informed medical predictions to the contrary.

It could be argued that Norman Cousins would have recovered anyway without laughter therapy. His particular case could be considered not scientifically significant since it is the account of only one person's experience. However, Mr. Cousins's conviction is clear in his book: laughter played a critical role in his recovery. Increasingly, evidence would suggest that his conclusion rests on a legitimate foundation.

The healing benefits of laughter are now well documented. When we laugh, rapid rhythmical contractions occur in the diaphragm. These contractions give the liver and the abdominal organs what amounts to a vibratory massage, stimulating their functions and activating digestive secretions. Contractions also occur in the musculature of the face, helping to relax tight jaw and cheek muscles.

Laughter causes us to breathe more rapidly, bringing more oxygen into our systems and accounting for the general feeling of euphoria that accompanies a good laugh. When we stop laughing, our blood pressure levels and heart rate drop below prelaugh levels. We feel more rested and relaxed. Immuglobulen A, a virus fighter found in our saliva, gets a temporary boost with laughter, which also causes the brain to release endorphins, the chemical agents that inhibit pain and generate feelings of well-being.[2]

As our bodies relax, so do our minds. Mental tensions lessen when laughter diverts the mind from problems and cares. The wise old doctor in Tom Sawyer recognized the linkage:

> ". . . the old man laughed loud and joyously, shook up the details of his anatomy from head to foot, and ended by saying that such a laugh was money in a man's pocket, because it cut down the doctor's bills like everything."[3]

Not only is laughter money in our pockets, but by learning to poke fun at our problems, we can gain mastery over situations that otherwise threaten to diminish us. This is Sylvia's great gift. It's not easy coping with a spouse who demands over and over, day in and day out, to know why we are in *their* house, refusing to believe we are their marriage partner, in spite of all the sacrifices we make to give them total care. Sylvia uses humor to keep her frustrations at bay. She tells her husband that she's his housekeeper, and her husband accepts that answer with none of the belligerence he demonstrates when she tries to convince him she is his wife.

It may well be that the pinnacle of mental health is the ability to laugh at the objects of our worries. If so, Sylvia scores high. By being humble in her faith and superior in her joy, she has found a way to keep a difficult life in proportion. Sylvia's designer genes are far more than just a good fit; for those of us who give care, they are worthy of cloning.

NOTES

1. Norman Cousins, *Anatomy of an Illness* (New York: Norton, 1979).

2. Ibid.

3. Mark Twain, *Mississippi Writings* (New York: Library of America, 1982), p. 103.

13

Chicken Noodle Soup and
Hot Chocolate with Marshmallows

"The fact of the matter is," Don tells the group, **"I can't give you a full report of how the evening went, I walked out long before it was over. I got tired of being talked at. I got tired of looking at graphs. I got tired of hearing how caregivers 'should' deal with their anger and depression. He made it sound so easy. Hell! The man may have a Ph.D., but he has never been a full-time caregiver."**

Don's report of a widely advertised lecture on caregiver stress put to rest the disappointment other members of the group felt at not having been able to attend. The evening of course, had been well-meaning. Most such evenings are. Experts come. Experts talk. Caregivers come. Caregivers listen.

> How to handle depression.

> How to talk so others will listen.

> How to give only to the point of resentment.

There appears to be no lack of answers for the dilemmas caregivers face. Increasingly we are being identified as an at-risk population; our areas of need are studied and educational outreach programs are mounted on our behalf. We "should" be grateful.

Don was not.

It took a mixture of courage and disgust for Don to walk out of the lecture. The particulars of his situation are complex. They do not lend themselves to graphs or well-meaning advice. Concerns of caregivers, when reduced to formulas and advice-giving is little more than patronization under the guise of helpfulness. No caregiver needs to be patronized. We are patronized enough as it is.

The fate love has undergone in our society is one of reduction. Persons have become objects to be studied, subjects to be administered to. All too often in the helping professions, helpfulness becomes a way to exercise power and control. What needs to be supportive presence is all too often a presence of directives, formulas, instruction, and advice-giving. Analysis and graphs replace respect and receptivity. Helpfulness becomes hindrance:

> **I'll be loving you always**
> **With a love that's true, always.**
> **When the things you've planned**
> **Need a helping hand,**
> **I will understand,**
> **Always.**
> **Days may not be fair, always**
> **That's when I'll be there, always.**
> **Not for just an hour,**
> **Not for just a day,**
> **Not for just a year,**
> **But always.**

The guest speaker, a music therapist, leads caregiver group members in the song of his selection. He then asks those present to write about how they show their love for the person they take care of and how that person, in return, shows their love for them. He is unaware that the exercise will be one of absolute futility for most in attendance.

Marlene sits wiping away tears. Her husband will soon no longer "always" be with her. Not only is a sentimental song inappropriate for Marlene, it is intensely painful.*

Barbara withdraws tightly into herself, blocked. Exhausted by eighteen years of "always" being there as a caregiver, she needs no reminder of the hours, days, years of her love.

Don's face tightens with frustration. His "always" commitment has kept him from living the kind of life he wanted for himself.

Others of the caregivers find the song and accompanying exercise

---

*Some days later Marlene's husband will die. The group will not see her again.

tension producing. Only one of the members is able to enter wholeheartedly into the venture.

The therapeutic effects of music are many. Our bodies are musical in themselves; complete rhythmic systems form the beat of the heart and pulses to the circulation of the blood and the movement of the lungs. Like intricately crafted musical instruments, when we get out of tune, our natural rhythmic pattern is altered; we become ragged, jagged, agitated, and despondent.

Music, with its own rhythymic patterns can help retune us. Soothing music reduces blood pressure levels and relieves muscular tension. Vigorous music stimulates by increasing blood circulation, thereby energizing us. Inspirational music uplifts, imparting courage and restoring faith.[1]

But as much as music renews, it can also irritate. All of us have experienced music that grates on our nerves; music that causes tension rather than alleviating it. Unpleasant emotions can be triggered by music every bit as much as pleasurable ones. It was this reversal effect of music that most of the group members experienced.

Had the therapist been more familiar with the nature of caregiving, the musical experience could have been more beneficial. An afternoon of joyful, playful, inspiring music would have been far more appropriate. Members would have left feeling renewed rather than sorry they had come.

Caregivers' most common complaint about professional "helpers" is that too many do not listen. They do not take the time necessary to fully understand the reality of those they attempt to assist.

The complaint is a legitimate one. As our society has become more technically oriented, interactions between people have become increasingly impersonal. Professional distance is the norm, not the exception. Professionals themselves are often the first to recognize the problem of remaining open and humanly available to those they seek to help. Still, many elect to keep their emotional distance and administer from a position of "expertise" rather than compassionate understanding.

It is not just professionals who are guilty. We all are.

"Everyone is so good at telling me what I should be doing differently, including my own children," Sylvia speaks out in frustration. "No one seems to have the time to really listen and fully understand what I am putting up with. If they did, maybe I would actually get some appreciation for what I do."

We who give care do not need to be preached at. More than likely we are doing the best that we can under the circumstances. We make mistakes. We get tired, cranky, and cross. We would like to meet everyone's ideal of caregiving. But we can't. We carry enough guilt as it is without having to fail those expectations others would heap upon us; others who probably could not follow their own advice if they had to serve in our place.

Music therapists, doctors, sons, parish workers: LISTEN. Hear our struggles. Hear our triumphs. Hear our needs. Hear our fears. Recognize that advice without experience is gratuitous. Give it to somebody else. Give *us* affirmation and acceptance. Let us educate you first. Then you can help to better educate us. We have priority needs that remain unmet. And they don't have to do with better job performance.

"It's not the responsibilities and never-ending demands that get to me. It's that my mother is not my mother anymore. I'm hers." Cynthia looks around somewhat embarrassed as she continues. "She was always the one who made me feel special. Now she hardly knows who I am, and the problem is . . . there's no one else in my life who makes me feel special."

Mothers nurture. Mothers soothe. Mothers hold. Mothers rock. Mothers stir up chicken noodle soup and hot chocolate with marshmallows. It is the mothering instinct in women and men that reaches out to make others feel special. That instinct is strong in those of us who give care. But we need mothering ourselves in return. Who comes around with soup and hot chocolate for us? Not our infirm family members. Their hands are unsteady. Not the advice-givers. They are too busy talking.

"I would say it's time we stop complaining about the lack of understanding we are receiving from our friends and family and everybody else." Donna pauses to look around her. "The reality is we are not going to get the care we need from others. It seems to me, we need to start figuring out how we can be more effective in giving care to one another."

Donna speaks responsibly. To wait and wish for others to stir the pot denies our own creative possibilities.

The age we live in is a narcissistic one, complicated by high degrees of stress and fear. People look out for themselves, not so much for one another. There is a place for faulting family members, friends, and professionals who lack sensitivity to our needs, but not if blaming is done to escape our own lack of responsiveness to others in situations similar to our own. Can we be counted upon to help other caregivers to cope with the diminishments of caregiving?

Support groups mature into supportive communities when their attending caregivers recognize that there is more to support than meeting together in formal sessions. Needs for chicken noodle soup do not fall just on specific days in specified time frames. Like Cynthia, we who give care need to know that we are special . . . and on a regular basis.

Members of support groups who weld themselves into viable communities do so because they reach out to one another as need decrees, not as clocks dictate. They find their "specialness" in solidarity, reaching out to one another.

They call one another in between sessions.

It is "special" to talk with someone who understands and cares enough to call.

o O o

They give emotional support and immediate presence when emergencies arise in any of their lives.

It is "special" to have a shoulder to lean on . . . to cry on.

o O o

They go out to lunch, engage in recreational activities together, and socialize in one another's homes as opportunities present themselves.

It is "special" to have friends with whom to laugh and play.

o O o

They keep track of birthdays.

It is "special" to be remembered and celebrated on one's birthday.

o O o

They share photographs of their infirm family members.

It is "special" to have others show an interest in the ones you love.

o O o

When resource people come, they tape the meeting for those absent.

It is "special" to know others think about you when you are not present.

o O o

They check up on one another when someone fails to attend a meeting.

It is "special" to know you have been missed.

o O o

They hold one another accountable for lifestyle changes any one of them is attempting to make.

It is "special" to know that others give backing and help strengthen resolve.

This is the kind of support and commitment Donna is suggesting. Her group has not yet come this far, attempts have been made but not followed up on. Whether they will become a true supportive community cannot be determined at this point in time. Caring for an infirm family member stretches the heart to its limits. How does one stretch it even further to include other needful human beings other than when it is convenient?

There is no answer for the "how," no formula to advance. "Do unto others as you would have them do unto you" is patronizing advice when the going seems so totally impossible for a multitude of legitimate reasons . . . beginning with exhaustion.

What, then, can be said to caregivers who know they can and must be more to one another than polite appearances, sharing frustrations and hugs on a periodic basis? Only this. First find one another's hands and hold them tightly. Laugh together, cry together. Take time for play and recreation. Don't let meetings end by the clock. Stay vigilant at the soup pot. We have to learn to love something before we can take proper care of it: people or pets, caregivers or pots of petunias. Hearts stretch further as they are ready. Love is the great adept.

"I always hesitate to call people because I think I have to be Mrs. Fix-it," Barbara tells the group. "But I have been a caregiver long enough to know that most caregiver problems can't be fixed, so I don't call. Then last week Doris phoned just to see how I was getting along. Her call meant the world to me. She is up to her eyebrows in problems of her own, yet she still took the time to check up on me. We didn't try to fix anything. We visited. We laughed. We cried on each other's shoulder. And you know what? When we hung up, I felt there wasn't anything the rest of the day I wouldn't be able to handle!"

NOTE

1. Shelly Katch, *The Music Within You* (New York: Simon and Schuster, 1985).

14

Barbara Larsen

Spiritual Darkness and Light, and the Importance of Support Systems

"Caregiving has been my life for over eighteen years. First my mother had to be nursed with cancer. I went to be with her in Seattle and stayed with her nine months until she died. It was a very difficult time. Then we brought my father, who was suffering with emphysema, up to Portland to live with us. One of our living areas was transformed into a hospital room for him. He died with us, very slowly and painfully. Shortly thereafter I was diagnosed with cancer. It was a lymphoma that had wrapped itself in some way around my spine. Surgery came first, then chemotherapy. But the chemotherapy was not effective in the way the doctors thought it would be, and they told me to get my affairs in order because I could not expect to live. I remember being less concerned about dying than about living well during the time I had left. The medication together with the prayerful support of my daughter and many others resulted in a miraculous turnaround; the cancer went into remission. To this day, almost sixteen years later, all I have are some residual traces along my spine.

"About the time I recovered from the cancer, my husband was stricken with severe rheumatoid arthritis. As his condition worsened, a whole host of complications set in. He now lives in constant pain and has virtually no hip joints left on either side. He can support himself only to transfer from his wheelchair to the toilet, the bed, or his chair, and has to have oxygen after each such exertion. I have hospice help now; he is not expected to live much longer. But he has a strong fighting spirit and has already outlived all expectations.

"Both he and I agree that if it hadn't been for our faith during the last ten years, neither one of us could have survived. I imagine we would have become either alcoholic or suicidal.

"Don't mistake me. I am not one of your typical religious types who surrender wholeheartedly to God. I am rebellious and strong willed. I am not always faithful, and I do not cling to God like others I know. Often it seems like he is just not available to me. I know he is supposed to always be with us, but it doesn't seem to me that he is.

"I get tired of hearing that God will give me the strength to carry my cross. The fact is, I have gotten strength from God, but it's running out. I don't need Scriptural quotes; I need help and understanding. Why is it so hard to give someone who's hurting a hug and just listen to them? Giving advice, particularly spiritual advice, is so self-righteous. It's like saying, 'I have it together, why don't you?'

"Fortunately, I have a few close friends who do their very best to come to my aid. Once, a respected member of my church told me how he often felt empty and estranged from God. I decided I was in good company in my spiritual darkness!

"Mostly, I have given up trying to figure God out. What I do know is that we limit God too much. I may not share the close emotional connection with him others claim to have, but I do find God in Nature, in beauty, in happy memories, and in small miracles. Also, I am convinced that God works through others; for example, close friends and my caregiver support group. You can have old friends and very good ones, but no one can truly understand what you are going through unless they have experienced or are experiencing something similar themselves.

"A great part of the time I am so exhausted, I don't want to go anywhere but to bed. The exception I make is for my caregiver group. I'll make any amount of effort to go, there is such care in the group, such understanding. The times in between meetings, though, are too long. We should be getting together outside of meetings, even if just to have lunch once in a while.

"I love to eat out. Because most of my life is bound up in serving my husband in some way or another, I feel almost desperate to go out for a meal and be waited on. We used to eat out a lot. For the past few years it was the last outside pleasure we could share. Cabin fever would build up, and we would go out for lunch or dinner. But then 'Dear Abby' printed a letter written by someone who had a vendetta against disabled people eating in restaurants—the ones who eat messily. She said her family spent good money to go out, and it was disgusting to have to be in the same room with people who were revolting to look at.

"My husband saw the letter. After that he refused to go out again to eat. It was already embarrassing enough for him to eat out in public. It took a lot of courage. He can only get food to his mouth by having a spoon tied on his wrist. All of his movements are awkward, and things *can* get messy. But he is bound and determined to keep feeding himself. The letter, though, did beat him down a lot and left me furious. How dare a person judge by appearances!

"Looking at my husband now no one could know he survived Nazi captivity. He fought under General Patton, was captured, and spent six months in a German prison camp. All the prisoners had to eat was one bowl of potato soup daily, with some very few exceptions. They worked from sun up to sun down building railroad tracks for the German trains. Many died. Only a sheer act of will kept my husband going. He returned home to be a dedicated employee, a wonderful husband, and a good father. Even now, he allows nothing to keep him down. He has adapted tools so he can make cedar chests for all the girls in the family. He works slow but he never gives up. People like my husband—disgusting? No. The woman who wrote to Abby is disgusting.

"Anyway, that's why we don't go out to eat anymore. And the loneliness of being housebound is compounded by the fact that few former acquaintances come to see us. I know people think we aren't much fun to be with. We can't go places and share in activities. It's really hard to keep up your spirits when so much is denied to you. Often I don't feel cheerful, but I've learned to keep up a good front most of the time. My husband would get frightened if he knew the toll caregiving has taken on me. I keep nearly everything bottled up inside, unless I am with my caregiver group. I don't know what I would do without them.

"Not too long ago, I accused my husband of being a jerk because that is the way he was acting. And then I started to laugh because it felt so good to stop being Miss Sunshine and actually say what was on my mind!

Both Barbara and her husband have drawn deeply on their faith to sustain them through the stressful years of illness. Like many other people of faith, prayer has been their line of defense as crises multiplied.

Increasing documentation seems to validate what religious people like Barbara and her husband have long recognized: faith and prayer can be of immense help in coping with pain, difficulty, and stress. Herbert Benson, M.D., an associate professor of medicine at Harvard Medical School, is one of a growing number of investigators who are studying the effects of prayer on health and stress reduction. As author of the long-time best seller, *The Relaxation Response,*[1] Dr. Benson advocates a very simple method of relaxation. The method consists of sitting quietly in a comfortable position and breathing slowly and deeply, much as discussed on page 55, but with the addition of silently repeating a word or phrase that is correlated with the breath. In his earlier work, Dr. Benson believed neutral, soothing words would be most effective, words such as: "ocean," "one," and "peace" were recommended.

As his work progressed, he encouraged people to select a short word from their faith if they were so inclined. Some 80 percent did. And to Dr. Benson's surprise, those who used words associated with their faith not only made a more lasting commitment to their stress reduction program, but they demonstrated better results in terms of health.[2] Terming this unexpected finding the *faith factor,* Dr. Benson has concluded that for whatever reason, *faith does make a difference in enhancing the power of the mind over health and disease.*

Since those findings, Dr. Benson has reached many in his work: ministers, rabbis, nuns, and priests. He showed them how to achieve the relaxation response through prayer.[3] His books continue to circulate widely, offering instruction in how to use religious belief systems to become quiet, calm, and more assured.

The method is basically the same as in his early work, except the words selected to be repeated silently in combination with the breath must have religious connotations. He recommends that the words used in his technique be easy to pronounce and short enough to say silently while exhaling. When thoughts arise, as they always will, people are counseled to return quietly to the word of focus. Ideally the practice is done at one sitting for a minimum of ten minutes each day. It can also be used any time during the day or night when problems, stress, or emotional difficulties threaten to overwhelm.

Barbara would find Dr. Benson's work of interest. The "faith factor" would be her way of explaining why the cancer in her body went into remission. Much conjecture, of course, surrounds cancers in remission. Spiritual healing is only one of the many plausible explanations. Moreover, the power of faith is difficult to prove. Still, that is no reason to reject it out of hand. The sincerity of people coming together with shared beliefs may well have powerful effects upon those in need.

Such healing energies did not come into play for Barbara's husband, for whom prayer ministry was also enlisted. The fact that prayer did not lead to cure or abatement of his pain, however, has not been a deterrent to their faith. But although Barbara continues to believe spiritual healing was responsible for her cancer going into remission, of late, she has found it hard to accept God's ways. Her sense of the Divine is diminishing. The God upon whom she has leaned for so many years, increasingly seems to be less available to her to draw upon for strength and fortitude.

It takes courage for a person of faith to be willing to bear testimony to the perception of a failed God rather than a victorious one. It is also a mark of spiritual maturity to cling in faith to a God less present than the God others claim to know so intimately.

"We limit God too much," Barbara says, and she speaks of her experience of Presence in Nature, in beauty, in the gift of memory making, in small daily miracles. Spirit, to Barbara, draws especially close to us in human acts of care, concern, empathy, respect, and love. She finds God mirrored in others, and even more strongly when groups of people join together to give support.

Certainly there is healing potential in a group, especially in those whose members have moved beyond the narrow limits of self-interest into a genuine sharing of one anothers' burdens. To experience care and appreciation while simultaneously having the opportunity to vent pent-up feelings helps reduce mental and emotional tensions. As people relax, feelings of well-being are generated.

Physicists verify that energy is amplifed when people come together in a collective way. The whole is literally greater than the sum of its parts. Most of us have had the experience of feeling devoid of energy because of tiredness, discouragement, and depression, only to then become energized when joining with others in situations resonant with joy, laughter, and compassion. It is as though the lower-energy vibration loses its charge by being absorbed into the higher energetic field.

Just as people who gather together in anger and righteousness become a lynch mob, those gathering together in support of one another become a healthier whole. Not that the mere gathering of human beings guarantees a heightened energy potential. Not all angry groups become mobs; not all support groups promote a greater sense of well-being or healing for their membership. What can be said, however, is that the potential for constructive, uplifting energy is generally greater in groups than is the case individually. Persons coming together, whether in shared concern or in prayer, evoke a natural energetic principle as uplifting as it is encompassing.

Barbara does not seek explanations for miracles. She does, however, see it as miraculous when people care enough about one another to be of ongoing help and support.

Those of us who give care spend a good deal of our lives giving such help and support. But just as batteries wear down and need to be recharged, so do we. Some of us may be able to recharge by ourselves on our own. Voltage requirements differ. Most of us, though, need to draw on more inclusive currents.

Religious communities have always counseled people in times of need to reach out for Divine support. Barbara, however, would contend that divine support comes to us also *through* human support. It is in community that she finds the healing vitality once encountered in her more private times of prayer. And who is to say but that her God is not so withdrawn after all. Perhaps in some mystical way God *is* actually drawing closer, in the smiles, embraces, precious understandings, and mischievous, joyful laughter of Barbara's fellow human beings.

NOTES

1. Herbert Benson, M.D., *The Relaxation Response* (New York: Avon, 1975).

2. Herbert Benson, M.D., *Beyond the Relaxation Response* (New York: Time Books, 1984).

15

Suffering

Eleven caregivers gather on a rainy, cold, November day, the outside dreariness mirroring the inside despair.

Three caregivers are edging close to breakdown.

Two caregivers are courting defeat due to recent complications in already overwhelming responsibilities.

One caregiver is resorting to antidepressants to get through her days with some measure of equanimity.

One caregiver is struggling to determine whether she has indeed reached the limits of her caregiving abilities.

Long pauses of silence characterize the meeting. What help is offered is largely wordless.

There simply *are* times in life when suffering is too intense to diffuse, even within a circle of friends or family who care deeply. Efforts to subvert the pain are futile and ultimately disrespectful. Each of the caregivers in pain has a personalized process to live through, which their friends, as much as they may want to, cannot truly fathom. Yet, because all present are bound by the common experience of caregiving, comfort is available. Arms find their way around shoulders. Hands reach out to hold. Eyes are moist with compassion.

To provide simple presence is one of the most difficult of all caring acts. To be present while family or friend cries in the knowledge that there is nothing one can do is excruciating: sitting, watching, listening while another's heart breaks. Yet, being silently open to another person's suffering, extraordinarily difficult as that may be, is a potentially profound experience. To be able to do so is to enter into the wordless, transformative realm of extraordinary communication and sharing; a realm that can make it possible to bear together what is too difficult to bear alone.

Viktor Frankl, a European born psychiatrist, has written at length about the experience of suffering, primarily because, as a Jew interned in German concentration camps, he was a witness to so much suffering, including his own. As the months and years of camp life passed, he became haunted by the fact that prisoners who endured under such brutally agonizing conditions usually differed from those who did not. Trained as a therapist to probe, he set about finding out why.

Survivors, it turned out, had an amazing will to live, in spite of the brutal suffering to which they were subjected. To be starved, beaten, tortured, and driven beyond what it seems the human spirit can endure and still survive seems unthinkable. Survivors were not necessarily physically robust, nor did education, status, or religious devotion set them apart. What did? The ability to derive *meaning* from their lives.

Frankl drew on the works of the German philosopher Friedrich Nietzsche who had written at length about meaning. "He who has a *why* to live can bear with any *how*."[1] Life in the concentration camps gave credence to Nietzsche's thought. Prisoners who had intensely held reasons to live were far more likely to survive than those who did not.

Strongly held values turned out to be life-supporting. Deep, abiding love kept many prisoners alive. These were persons who lived to be reunited with family members or struggled to remain alive so they could shepherd those family and friends in their care.

Meaning for others came from compassionate outreach to fellow prisoners in need. The annals of concentration camp life are filled with acts of heroism: people risking and sacrificing for one another at great personal cost. Close to starvation themselves, there were those who gave up their meager rations of food to others who also desperately needed food to survive. There were those who gave up clothing and coverings at peril to their own bodies. Many inmates endured unspeakable hardships and/or died making life possible for family members or friends.

Placing our own lives in jeopardy for the sake of others is not an instinct with which we are born. Why some are able to engage in selfless acts and others are not remains a subject about which there can be only speculation. None of us can know how we would respond in similar situations.

It is excruciating to read about the concentration camps or watch documentaries about them. Even so, second-hand experience lacks any real comprehension of the enormity of the suffering so many thousands endured. What is remarkable is that meaning could be found in the midst of such suffering. Frankl's writings serve as testament to those prisoners for whom suffering became a means to deepen in faith.

Unspeakable horrors continued unabated: wrongs were not righted, cruelty was not mitigated, prayers went unanswered, and hope seemed nonexistent. And although many of us will be unable to comprehend how people could possibly intensify in trust and faith under such circumstances, the wonder is that there were those who did and who, in so doing, *found a strength that sustained their will to live.*

Frankl's observations and experiences so altered him that upon his release, he formulated a new school of psychotherapy called logotherapy; "logo" coming from the Latin word for "meaning." His book *Man's Search for Meaning* is the account of his concentration camp experiences, along with an introduction to logotherapy. Having gone through many printings, this work continues to be inspirational reading for millions who seek ways to cope with their suffering.

There is nothing positive that can be said about the horrors of concentration camps except this: *prisoners were in a community of suffering.* While there were always some prisoners who were isolated from the group, most lived and died together. As is always true in group life, there were those despicable acts of human nature perpetrated by some of the prisoners themselves. But these stood in stark contrast to the acts of human decency: the care, compassion, outreach, and sport that kept untold numbers alive and enabled others to die less broken.

A somewhat similar phenomena has been written about by the Van Ornums in their book *Talking to Children about Nuclear War.*[2] These authors reference studies of children being reared in war-torn environments: children in communities under constant siege where death and suffering are everyday occurrences. The studies reveal an astounding fact. Many of the children evidence none of the expected symptoms of acute stress and suffering: neurosis, night terrors, or shock. They remain impervious to what most of us would find unbearable.

Why? Parents and extended family, together with a tightly integrated community, provide the children with *maximum amounts of love* in spite of the surrounding madness.

If people in brutally malignant circumstances are able to make enormous contributions to the emotional well-being of one another, why can't we? Certainly the ideal for caregivers in the throes of stress would be to have others close at hand to provide strength and caring presence. But many of us do not. Even those of us with family members living in close proximity often are unable to procure the ongoing support, help, and understanding we need. Reality being what it is, what can be said to comfort those of us who must suffer in silence because there is no circle of care present?

The few words that can be said center around courage. There is no condition of life in which we are more alone than that of suffering. When we do not have the simple, caring presence of others there can be no temporary easing of pain save through the intervention of drugs or the relief of sleep. The remainder of the time, suffering annihilates any possibility of peace or positive thinking, thus keeping us submerged in agony.

To confront agony and not be lessened and demeaned by it takes enormous courage. Suffering cannot be wished away any more than it can be appeased. Suffering extracts its pound of flesh, day after day, week after week. For some of us, year after year.

Mercilessly, suffering will diminish us if we let it, relentlessly forcing us into postures that are pathetic, narrowly self-serving, sometimes stridently ugly. Suffering never gives in; it is too savage to be conciliatory.

It is only with courage that we can make a stand. Dignity best characterizes the stand courage takes. To suffer courageously is to recognize that resentment is useless and struggle is futile. Courage recognizes that there is more to suffering than smallness of person. It will not allow the glorification of pain any more than it will the nursing of wounds or internalization of the role of "victim." One of the greatest tests of life is to bear defeat without losing heart. Courage challenges us to be worthy of suffering's claim upon us.

"I believe that I know and share the many sorrows and searing circumstances that a human being can experience, but I do not cling to them; I do not prolong such moments of agony. They pass through me, like life itself, as a broad, eternal stream. They become part of that stream, and life continues. And as a result, all my strength is preserved; it does not become tagged on to futile sorrow or rebelliousness."[3]

The speaker is not a Portland caregiver. The care she gave was to Jews in Auschwitz where she herself was a prisoner.[4] Why Etty Hillesum survived her suffering and others did not is unanswerable. And while the reason may have had something to do with her ability to let suffering pass through her; it may have had nothing to do with her survival. Nonetheless her words are instructive. What she demonstrates is resilience and a willingness to take responsibility for what she did have of her life, despite her extreme suffering. That is courage.

So is this: It takes courage to recognize that suffering may lead to meaning. It takes courage to recognize that suffering may *not* lead to meaning. Courage recognizes that there are no assurances with suffering, except one: anguish. But there are *possibilities*. Hearts that have known pain have a way of expanding:

"I have to believe all these years have prepared me to be more than I could have been otherwise." Barbara is imploring the group to begin a more comprehensive outreach of care and concern.

"We are the ones who know firsthand how hard caregiving can be; no one knows better than we what caregivers need and how to give it. We've *got* to do a better job of reaching out to one another. We've got to do a better job of reaching out to all the caregivers in this community who don't have a clue how to begin getting the support that they need. What else, really, are we here for? I can't speak for the rest of you, but I'm not about to let these years of suffering be in vain!"

NOTES

1. Victor Frankl, *Man's Search for Meaning* (New York: Pocket Books, 1985).

2. Ibid.

3. William Van Ornum and Mary Wickett, *Talking with Children about Nuclear War* (New York: Continuum Press, 1984).

4. *An Interrupted Life: The Diaries of Etty Hillesum, 1941–43* (New York: Pantheon Press, 1984), p. 81.

16

Donna Alfano

The Importance of Music
and Inspirational Aids

"When I think back over the last twenty-two years, it seems like my family and I have been on a boat that didn't get very far off shore before it capsized. Ever since then, the boat has been drifting out to sea with all of us hanging on the sides for dear life. My hold seems to be the one getting weaker and weaker. If there isn't a rescue soon, I'm afraid I am going to slip off and go under.

"Right after we married, things started to go wrong with my husband's health. His behavior became more and more erratic. He kept losing jobs. When we finally got the diagnosis of multiple sclerosis (MS), it explained a lot of things. Apparently, the disease had its onset way before we were married but the symptoms had never been correctly diagnosed.

"Initially, I thought some of my husband's mental confusion was more related to the stress of a growing family and his inability to hold down a job. When we married I accepted the responsibility for his two small daughters from a previous marriage. They were raised along with our own three children. Usually MS affects the body, not the mind. With my husband it was both. Once that was established, we had the explanation for his uncharacteristic behaviors.

"The years before he was correctly diagnosed and able to get help were horrible. To this day I try to keep them blocked out of my mind. The one thing that kept me going was my love for the children. I was determined that they would be raised with some sort of normalcy to their lives. They had a right to grow up with as little scarring as possible from their father's illness.

"It was just a year ago that we finally moved him to a retirement home; his disease had progressed to the point where we couldn't keep him with us. The move solved some problems but created a lot of new ones. He is alert, and yet at the same time confused. He doesn't understand why he was moved, and he resents me terribly. A good deal of my time is still taken up with his needs: trying to find ways of communicating so he can make sense of his world, running interference between all the professionals involved with his case, and battling the bureaucratic structure of the Veterans' Administration.

"The time that doesn't go to my husband goes to my children and trying to keep up with the housekeeping responsibilities. There have been a lot of caregiving responsibilities for my parents as well. Often it seems to me miraculous that I am all in one piece because I have been pulled in so many directions for so long. I compare myself to a rechargeable battery. Even though I get worn down, I always get the energy to go back. And yet like rechargeables, each new charge doesn't last as long. Right now I feel very, very dim. I often wonder if I am finally going to break. At this point of my life, I am so worn down from all the years of caregiving that I'm not sure I would even recognize the impending signs of a breakdown.

"Part of my problem may be that I am so conscientious. I work overtime to be both a father and mother to my children. My husband gets a lot more of my time than other wives might give their husbands under similar circumstances. But I keep thinking what it would be like if the tables were turned and I was the helpless one. Over the years he has become like another one of my children. The big difference is he is never going to grow up, and his care needs can go on for another twenty or thirty years.

"Friends tell me to make a new life for myself. I don't see any way right now to do that. I am not divorced and do not plan to be, even though sometimes it seems I will have to make some kind of major break, or I am going to end up pretty sick myself.

"I know enough about stress to know you have to have coping strategies or it wears you down to the point of chronic illness, maybe even premature death. So I do what is in my power to do. For example, this year I planted more flowers than I ever have before. So much of my time is spent taking care of others that what I need most is alone time just for myself. Some friends of mine think I need to get out more, but I don't think they understand how much more I can relax when I am alone.

"The caregiver support group isn't always productive for me. All the members are older than I am; all have had reasonably fulfilling lives before becoming caregivers. They didn't start young and grow with it into middle age as I have. I feel cheated of most of my life. It would help me to be around other women in my situation. I have read about such women, but I don't know any in person.

"Music comes more to my rescue than people. We have a piano in our home. I love playing it, although it seems I don't get the opportunity very often. The hard part about putting out so much of myself for others is that I'm not left with enough time to do the things I want to do just for myself. Some of that is the fault of my priorities, but other times I have no other choice.

"When I do our grocery shopping, I go to a large store that has a grand piano in its delicatessen area. Customers can sit down and play any time they wish. I know the hours and days when two elderly gentlemen come to play. Both are excellent pianists and play the kind of music I enjoy. As much as I can, I plan my grocery shopping around the times one or the other is playing. I do my marketing first, then I sit down at one of the tables and stay as long as possible. I used to detest marketing as just one more chore. I don't anymore. Now it's my free therapy session!!

"I don't want to lose my hold on that sinking boat. The thing of it is, I may not have a choice. The other image that I can't get out of my head is of being in a long dark tunnel. There is a light at the end, but not the light of release people like to talk about. The light at the end of the tunnel is from an oncoming train, and it seems to me that it is going to crush me in its path.

"Maybe that is morbid thinking. Maybe it is a true premonition. I honestly don't know. I do know that when such thoughts set in, along with depression and despair, I have to break their hold or I will be crushed.

"That's one of the reasons I keep all kinds of inspirational materials close at hand. When things get black, I sit and read until I feel better. Other times I will put on one of my tapes. The ones I like best are from people who have overcome tremendous odds in their lives. Their stories give me hope. I want to believe that my story will have a happy ending someday. But if it doesn't, then I want the ending to be courageous. I want to know I kept on struggling against the odds right up until the train runs me down."

"Stress" is the name of the train, and it can be a ruthless juggernaut. Donna's analogy of the rechargeable battery is a poignant one. Years and years of unrelenting stress have already taken a large toll on her life. As Donna well knows, chronic illness and often premature death are among the consequences of prolonged stress. But whether or not stress will finally claim her as a victim cannot be known at this time.

The great paradox of stress is how some people are able to bear up under it while others become casualties. Like many of the surviving concentration camp inmates, it is the "meaning" she assigns to life that partly explains how Donna has weathered over twenty years of a highly stressful existence. She has put herself in service to the love she has for family. Difficult as that has proven to be, Donna will have it no other way.

Genetic make-up may also play a role. Some people are constitutionally stronger and more able to physically withstand stress than others. Whether she knows it or not, Donna may be a member of this hearty group.

Then, too, Donna has her "lifelines": her flowers, her music, and her inspirational materials. The train may be coming down the track, but Donna is not cowering in its path. She is doing what she can to slow down its travel time.

Music is a particularly good choice. Years ago, the therapeutic value of music was widely recognized. Egyptians called music the doctor of the soul. Egyptian priest-physicians used it in many of their healing practices. Persians played music on the lute to cure various illnesses, most of which were likely stress related. Hebrews used harp music for the same purposes. Confucius believed music was necessary for harmonious living. Plato said listening to music could help keep bodies and minds healthy.

Such ancient practices may seem simplistic in this age of medical high technology. Yet, mothers everywhere instinctively know to rock and sing softly to fussy, out-of-sorts babies, restoring balance and rhythm to agitated states. Like intricately created musical instruments, when we get out of tune, our natural rhythmic pattern is altered. We who are caregivers know those times well. Unlike babies, however, we cannot be rocked back to well-being. But because there is such a strong relationship between music and emotions, we can restore ourselves to more harmonious rhythms.

Research into the therapeutic use of music has intensified since the 1970s when stress became a household word. Not so surprisingly, studies of music's potential for stress reduction confirm what ancient practitioners knew: music heals.[1]

Carefully designed sedative listening studies measuring the soothing effects of music on blood pressure demonstrate a decrease in both systolic and diastolic rates.[2] We don't have to have our blood prsesure checked to realize how much better listening to soothing music can make us feel. But a keener appreciation of the relationship between music and health may encourage us to incorporate music more frequently into our lives, especially during those times when stress is particularly high.

Muscle tension is also eased by flowing, soothing tones. Many of us turn on the television when we want to relax. The phonograph or radio may be a better choice. Mental stimulation may get our mind off our concerns, but mental stimulation does not generate the kind of brain wave patterns that correspond to more therapeutic rest and relaxation.*

Donna takes her musical interludes on her marketing days. Others of us, with less travel time, can put on a record, a cassette, a compact disc. Our choices should and will vary. There is no "right" selection. To achieve music's therapeutic effects, what we listen to must have individual appeal. Some of us will lean to classical music, others to jazz. Hymns are a favorite selection, as are "golden oldies" and show tunes. The only guideline is personal preference.

Music stimulates every bit as much as it relaxes. Vigorous music increases blood circulation and enhances muscular strength and endurance. Throughout the country, aerobic classes capitalize on this feature of music with a beat. Factory managers have found employee productivity increases when lively music is played over sound systems.[3]

When we are feeling fatigued and do not want to exceed our caffeine limits, we might want to consider putting on a brisk piece of music. March tunes are particularly stimulating. It is hard to remain sluggish when a John Philip Sousa record is playing.

Just as music connects deeply with our emotional and physical nature, so does it connect with our spiritual nature. Since the beginning of time, music and worship have gone hand in hand. Both draw people together. Both provide a sense of comfort, support, nurturance, and bonding. Together they serve as primary defenses against fear and loneliness and have been used by all peoples from all times for that purpose. One of the best examples of the combined use of music and

---

*See page 92.

religion to comfort a community through adversity are the spirituals of enslaved blacks.

Caregiving, like slavery, often feels like bondage, particularly when the inner strength and resolve to persevere become difficult to access. That is not to equate the despicable and tragic conditions endured by slaves with the tribulations of caregiving. Nonetheless, despair, discouragement, and futility can overwhelm us in times of trial and sorrow. The great value of music lies in its ability to resonate with our emotions and lift us up: consider the power of verses from "We Shall Overcome," "Go Tell It on the Mountain," or "Old Man River."

Behind, beneath, beyond all desperation, Old Man River keeps rolling along. He is continuity. He is strength. He is power. He is our assurance that there is something timeless and eternal, something greater than our pain, yet encompassing it.

Worn down as we may be, music has a way of wrapping around our hearts and binding up their aches. And unlike many distressed peoples, particularly in underdeveloped countries, we are able to play music at will by the flick of a switch in the privacy of our homes, or listen to it in concert halls, open air performance centers, churches, shopping malls, or in grocery stores.

The Greek thinker Pythagoras prescribed a daily regimen of music for his followers so they could stay in harmony with themselves, no matter what the fates set in motion. He instructed them to wake up to music, to work to music, to relax to music, to go to sleep to music. His advice is worth following in our modern age, particularly for those of us giving care who want to make each day as healthy and as healing as we can, for ourselves and for our loved ones.

Just as Donna uses music to lift her when she is down, she seeks out other sources of inspiration as the need arises. Times of despair *are* bleak. They make us feel bereft and hopeless. Discouragement has a way of sapping vitality and creating a sense of misery so deep that we despair of ever extricating ourselves. It is as though we were not constitutionally designed to do battle in a vacuum with despondency. We need hope from others. Our responsibility is to acknowledge that fact and seek it out.

Because she does not have a close community of understanding friends from whom she can gain support, Donna does the next best thing. She surrounds herself with the inspirational works of others and listens to cassettes of those she admires who have triumphed over adversity.

It is not that Donna goes to inspirational materials to find answers for her problems. Worn, but wise from long years of caregiving, she knows there are no simple formulas for success. She recognizes that inspirational materials are not really meant for that purpose. Besides, Donna is aware that her own life may not have a happy ending. The ultimate reward for her sacrifices may be a nervous breakdown, chronic illness, or premature death. Regardless of what may lie ahead, Donna knows her challenge is to meet each day as it comes, doing the best she can, drawing on inspiration to help her as she falters.

To be inspired is to be infused with new life and possibility. When we are inspired, we feel aroused, stimulated, and animated. Originating with the notion of being filled with "spirit," to be inspired *is* to be in-spirited: raised up by forces stronger than our despair.

Breaking the hold of despair is not done with the shake of the head, a slap on the wrist, or an admonition to get our act together. It is done by something more life-giving: an elevation of our hearts and minds to possibility.

Each time we realize that we are not alone in our personal agonies, we are more able to transcend them. We need reminders that we belong to a common humanity, members of which likewise suffer and know defeat. Not only can the struggles of others be as fierce and as piercing as our own, some people endure much greater suffering. That others bear up and find ways to keep on *is* in-spiriting. We begin to recognize that we, too, are capable of more courage and resolve than we would have otherwise believed possible.

It is admirable and enviable when persons are able to turn adversity into personal triumph. Some do so through faith, others through will power, courage, or with the assistance of fellow human beings. Many such persons go on to write and speak about their experiences. Theirs are the materials with which Donna likes to surround herself.

People who become public inspirational figures have an important educational role to fulfill. So do those of us who succeed less spectacularly in triumphing over adversity but still refuse to become embittered and crippled by the pain.

Most of us stumble and lose our way, but we get back up and keep going. Our stories will not rivet an audience or sell scores of cassette tapes. But if we can learn to do a better job of sharing them with one another, we may be in less need of inspirational writings and tapes because we will have one another.

Donna's life of service would have taken less of a toll had she been able to lean on, share, and find support among other caregivers. As it is, the metaphors she uses to describe herself would seem to indicate that she is fast reaching her limit. She recognizes the potential for impending disaster unless she can make major changes in her caregiver situation. At this point she is not willing to make them. Maybe she cannot, for much the same reason a coal miner courting black lung disease cannot stop going down into the mines because his family has no other means of support. There are those times when destiny seems to take its course, fair or unfair as it may seem.

Even so, Donna is not one to cower. Her intent is to keep mustering the strength and resolve to keep from losing her grip on the capsized boat for as long as she can. The love she has for her family, her flowers, her music, and her inspirational tapes has helped solidify that hold for longer than could be expected under the circumstances.

Whether she knows it or not, courage has made Donna's own life an inspiration to many, regardless of its final outcome. Should she go down, it won't be with a whimper. We can only assume that it will be with a sigh of relief, knowing she has given her all for what she believes in.

NOTES

1. Katch, *The Music within You.*
2. Edward Podolsky, *Music Therapy* (New York: Philosophical Library, 1954).
3. Ibid.
4. Ibid.

17

The Final Integration

"As the time drew nearer for my mother to die, I had to place her in a long-term-care facility. With cancer spreading throughout her lungs and larynx, suctioning had to be done by professionals on a daily basis. She got excellent care where she was, and she was the first to acknowledge it. Nonetheless, she grew increasingly agitated as the days went by."

Russ is speaking about the closing days of his mother.

"I finally asked her if there was anything I could do to relieve her agitation. She told me she needed to return to her home for an afternoon to sit with her violets. I thought she was homesick and agreed. I had decided not to put her home on the market until after she died and had kept everything the way she had left it. The staff was very cooperative, helping me make all the necessary arrangements to take her home for part of an afternoon.

"She was edgy on the way over; some of it was the pain, but not all of it. When we got there, she walked around a little, but mostly she wanted to be by herself, sitting in her rocking chair among her violet plants. She rocked for almost two hours. I left her alone.

"She was still in pain when the time came to return her to the care center, but she seemed a different person from when we arrived. She was peaceful. There was a steadying strength about her; she was calm. The next few days were without agitation, and although her pain intensified, she died peacefully within the week."

None of us can say with any certainty what Russ's mother experienced that afternoon among her violets. Nor can any of us say with any certainty what happens during those times when we, too, return to the sources of our strength; walking in Nature, laughing with friends, baking an apple pie. What we do know is that our energy shifts. Obstacles and limitations seldom have been overcome. What has changed is our ability to manage them.

There is an intuitive wisdom within all of us. We *know* what we need to do to take care of ourselves. We *know* what inner calls to heed: the call of violets, the call of model boats, the call of supportive communities, the call of prayer. To respect that inner knowing and to work with it needs to be a priority in life as well as in death.

Unable of her own accord to return to sources of her strength, Russ's mother became agitated. She was fortunate that her son recognized her reaction as a plea for help. Others of us, when estranged from sources of our strength become cross, anxious, angry, withdrawn, petty, tyrannical. Such behaviors serve as signals, alerting us that priorities need to be reordered in our lives. It is time to heed our inner calls; time to return to our violets.

Failing to do so, our choices are limited: blow up or burn out.

"Coping with Caregiving" is the group's topic of discussion. Their guest speaker, a ministerial counselor, urges all members present to remember how much they put out is the measure of how much they need to put back in.

"Output minus input equals burnout." Don paraphrases.

"Exactly!" the counselor nods his head in agreement. And when that happens, you have to find a gas pump, quick."

"What do you do when the pumps are all out of gas?" Sylvia rejoins.

Those present laugh . . . uncomfortably.

The counselor has no ready answer to provide.

Sometimes the most honest answer is no answer. But there is a place for cautions.

First caution:

Once we understand the absolute necessity of taking care of ourselves, most of us will probably attempt to do so, except when we are tired. Then most of us cannot.

Weariness and physical exhaustion can sabotage even the best of renewal programs and the strongest resolve. Tiredness depletes and discourages. When we lose the motivation to take care of ourselves, lack of adequate sleep may be the cause. Fatigue contaminates resolve depleting the energy needed to act on one's own behalf.

When tiredness is the culprit, emphasis needs to be placed on getting the rest we need. Once we are able to do that, we may discover that our gas pumps are not as depleted as we thought.

Sometimes, however, getting our sleep needs met is simply not possible. Home care of an infirm family member is not a convenience occupation. There are those nights when we are more up than down. Adrenalin surges and catnaps may be the only sources of our fuel, along with fortitude.

Second caution:

Barring those times when tiredness intervenes, we may not be getting gas from our pumps precisely because *we are not willing to pump to get it.* The forces of inertia and self-pity will sap every ounce of available energy we have *if* we allow them to do so.

Action, courage, motivation, strong resolve, and support from others are the antidotes for inertia and self-pity. None come by wish or whim. Either we find the courage to do everything in our power to procure the help and support we need or we suffer the consequences. They will not be pretty ones.

The above cautions do not apply to Sylvia. She is a woman of courage; she takes risks for her health. She generally is able to get the rest her body needs. Her pumps have not always been dry. She has not allowed them to be. But increasingly, the choice does not seem to be hers.

Long years of struggle with no end in sight push Sylvia to the despair born of exhaustion. What counsel *can* be given under such conditions? Exercise more? Laugh more? Play more? Take more respite breaks? Identify better support systems?

The therapist attempted no such answers. Nor did he attempt inspirational counsel. With the kind of circumstances confronting Sylvia, well-meaning responses and inspirational advice would provide no more lasting comfort than a Valium pill.

The hard reality is, some of us who give care will come to a place at which exercise, prayer, respite, humor, or inspiration can *no longer be counted upon to do the job.* And if we know in our hearts the time has not yet come to relinquish care, is there no hope for our despair?

There *is* hope. There is *always* hope if we are willing to keep pushing on. This is true even when there seems to be no promise of help. It is only by pushing on that we may encounter the *unexpected.* New sources of strength sometimes appear in the darkest of hours. In the midst of despair unanticipated support systems may come to our aid. The phone rings with a genuine offer of help; something for the better changes in our family member's condition.

There are, of course, no guarantees. The unexpected can never be planned for; none of us can anticipate when, where, or why there may be a shift in our favor. All that can be said is that when unexpected help does make its appearance in our lives, we go forward encouraged, able to bear up for one more hour, one more afternoon, one more sleepless night.

Overhead neons turned out, votive candles glow with unfailing light. Verses from *The Prophet* call group members back to timeless strength as Bill reads:

> **Then a woman said, "Speak to us of Joy and Sorrow."**
> **And he answered:**
> **"Your joy is your sorrow unmasked . . .**
> **How else can it be?**
> **The deeper sorrow carves into your being,**
> **the more joy it can contain."[1]**

Although not new to the group, Bill has been absent many months due to the heavy care demands of his wife who died just a few days earlier, ending weeks of intense pain. Bill speaks simply and movingly of her closing days and of her death. It is he who has brought with him *The Prophet*, wanting to share its words of comfort.

> **Some of you say, "Joy is greater than sorrow,"**
> **and others say, "Nay, sorrows is the greater."**
> **But I say unto you they are inseparable.**
> **Together they come, and when one sits alone with you**
> **at your board, remember the other is asleep on your bed.**
> **Verily you are suspended like scales between**
> **your sorrow and your joy.**
> **Only when you are empty are you at standstill and balanced."[2]**

A quiet falls over the group. The caregivers sit silently for some minutes in the candlelight as a deep peace settles over the room.

The afternoon serves as a reminder that renewal is greater than the sum of its parts. As the group members sit in silence amid the glowing red votive lights bound by a stillness beyond suffering and joy, they are strengthened. It is a form of renewal members had not planned, did not expect, and made no effort to receive. It came unexpectedly, as a gift.

The unexpected has a way of doing that. The sun's rays at dusk suddenly erupt in colors of purple, azure, crimson, and gold. We breathe deeply and find ourselves relaxed. The bacon crisps to perfection. We smile in delighted surprise; the tight muscles in our face release their grip. A night of uninterrupted sleep leaves us rested and refreshed; we have the energy to renew our resolve to better meet *our* needs. Our infirm family member, usually cranky and self-absorbed, looks at us with moist eyes filled with unspeakable gratitude. We know we will carry on, even at great expense to ourselves.

Amid all the chaos and disruption caregiving brings to our lives, unexpected happenings have a way of coming as if to serve as reminders that there is a rightness to life in spite of its anguish.

The author of *The Prophet* makes a related point: *"The deeper sorrow carves into your being, the more joy it can contain."*

In the midst of sorrow, there *is* joy to be had—certainly for caregivers. Caregiving was not meant to be a joyless state. Reaching out to meet the deeply human needs of another person is an act worthy of celebration. It may not seem so because in between catheter changes, trips to the drugstore, and the preparation of special diets, we get depleted. And it is then that joy becomes elusive in our lives. But it need not remain so.

Joy is reclaimed each time we return to the sources of our strength. It is released through the endorphins that go coursing through our bodies as we walk, swim, laugh, and relearn how to play. It evidences itself in care, concern, and understanding when we join in the support of one another. It sings out in music. It embraces us in respite breaks. It comes unexpectedly in hugs.

And if joy still seems foreign to us because sorrow has the edge in our life, more thoughts of *The Prophet* on joy bear recollection: *". . . they (joy and sorrow) are inseparable. Together they come, and when one sits alone with you at your board, the other is asleep on your bed."*

Sleepers can be awakened, maybe not each and every time, but often enough. Forget the alarm clocks. The awakening hinges on our willingness to chart a new course for ourselves, neither casually nor grudgingly.

Joy responds to firmness of resolve, a twinkle in the eye, and help when need be from our drum majorettes. We would do well to remember that we are never far from their counsel. Joy is not one to stay under wraps once we begin to strut and sound our own whistles.

"I just hate my husband's filthy language," Eileen's voice, with its clipped and proper British accent is filled with indignation. "I find his foul pronouncements thoroughly disgusting. The doctor says some of it has to do with his stroke and damage to brain centers, but knowing that doesn't change anything. I absolutely detest four-letter words, whether there is reason for them or not. But I'm starting to get on top of it. When he can't see me, I hold up my second pinkie and shake it at him with a perfect vengeance. What's absolutely shocking is how jolly fine doing that makes me feel!"

NOTES

1. Kahil Gibran, *The Prophet* (New York: Knopf, 1952), pp. 29–30.
2. Ibid.

18

Doris Graffam

The Goodness of Life, and the Tears

"It's my heart, not my head, that I try to listen to when I have to make decisions. My heart said I needed to bring my husband home after he had been in a care facility for three months. He didn't once ask to come home; he knew how hard it would be for me. We talked about it for three weeks before we made the change. But the living room was already made into a bedroom. We had done that eight years ago when his special care needs began. Three years later, he required twenty-four-hour care, which continued until the last hospitalization and subsequent nursing home placement. So it wasn't that I didn't know what I was getting into when I decided to bring him home. I did.

"Part of my decision came from watching him get worse in the nursing home. Because the staff didn't walk with him often enough, he was losing what little ability he had to be mobile. Also, he was getting more and more confused and disoriented with the passage of time. I wasn't ready to let that kind of deterioration set in, not when I suspected it was more the result of institutionalization than actual decline.

"The other part of my decision had to do with our relationship itself. This is my second marriage. My first was long-enduring and unhappy. In contrast, this marriage, up until the time my husband got sick, was like living in never-never land. I was treated like royalty from the beginning of our courtship. In the twelve years before he became incapacitated, we traveled, entertained extensively, and shared deeply. I still have a closet of floor-length formals. Our home was filled with friends and great happiness. How could I let my husband languish in a nursing home, not getting the care he deserves after such a life together.

"Family, friends, and doctors strongly advised against bringing him home. 'I'll be the first to admit that I have made a mistake,' I told them. I have yet to make that admission. I learned to be a survivor in my first marriage. Those years taught me that life hands us the bad every bit as much as the good and we had better know how to handle both!

"Pride, I will admit, plays a role in my not letting others know how difficult caregiving can be for me. I keep everything to myself. Maybe that is why I have so many tears. But I always feel better after a good cry. Tears are my escape and help keep family and friends from knowing how used up and discouraged I get. They would say 'I told you so.' I don't need to be told that. When people ask how things are going, I always say fine. Often things *aren't* fine, but I'll be the last to let on. Besides I *knew* they weren't going to be fine. *That's the whole point.* Once you accept the fact that life is going to be difficult, you learn to reach deeper inside of yourself to find ways to keep on keeping on.

"The biggest change that has occurred since bringing my husband home has been my level of tension: it's much higher now. Even though I have an excellent live-in housekeeper/aide to help me five days a week, the care demands are much greater than they were before. I am continually worried about my husband falling. He is a large man. I have to use a belt to help transfer him. It's actually costing us more to have him home than to have him in a care facility. There are a lot of financial decisions ahead that are adding enormously to my stress. Most of my tension centers in my back, shoulder, and neck areas. The knots there never seem to soften.

"I go to bed early in the evening, right after I put my husband down. I sleep for two or three hours and then get up and stay up for three or four hours in the middle of the night. It's my quiet time—all for me. No one makes demands and I have no schedules to follow. The house belongs to me. I bake bread. I iron. I pay bills. Making cream puffs is my midnight specialty. If I have a place to go the next day where people would like to get cream puffs, I bake them. Twice in the last two months, I've taken them to my caregiver support group.

"Everyone who is a caregiver needs to find some way of setting aside time just for themselves when they can do exactly what they want to do, when they want to do it. It just so happens that for me, that time is the middle of the night. Sometimes I am interrupted by my husband's needs but, by and large, the hours are my own. Those hours are not a luxury; they are an absolute necessity.

"Unless there is something I want to watch on late-night television, I usually have the radio on when I putter about. Music is a great help in lifting my spirits. I have played the piano ever since I was a little girl. Once I learned I could play by ear, I never was far from a piano or organ. Eventually I became quite a good accompanist, playing for fashion shows and other such events. When I remarried, I played a lot for our friends. We entertained quite a bit, and sing-alongs were always part of gatherings. We would even move my organ out on the patio so I could play for our large garden parties.

"My organ is difficult to get to now. We have had to rearrange the entire house around caregiving considerations. But although I don't play much myself anymore, music remains an important part of my life. I have season tickets to the Pops Orchestra; going to concerts is one way I spoil myself. I can be so tired the night of a concert that part of me just doesn't think I can make the effort to go. But I remember all the times I have been tired and chose to go anyway. I go even if I know I will probably doze off a bit during the performance. The last concert was a brass ensemble. I didn't doze through any of it! I came home all charged up and feeling worlds better than when I left.

"Nine months ago I had a brain aneurysm. It took something like that to show me how fragile and precious life is. We take so much for granted without realizing how fortunate we are, until it is too late. I am one of the lucky ones; I was given a reprieve. The aneurysm has made a big difference in the way I live my life. I don't dwell nearly as much on my problems. I look around me more and appreciate all I do have to be grateful for.

"People ask me if I worry about what's ahead for my husband and me. Since getting back on my feet, I have to say I worry a lot less than before. When I do think about the future, I think more about the clumps of violets that will be coming up all over the yard in the spring, the fragrance of lilacs that will be filling the air, and the fruit trees that will be in bud. Simple, life-giving pleasures; life is full of them!"

Doris recognizes that her close call with death showed life to be very fragile and very precious. Before being hospitalized, simple life-giving joys were more in the background. Now they are in the foreground.

Walking in her yard, Doris takes time to look at the silhouette of barren branches against the sky; she inspects the ground for signs of early bulbs. Donuts and coffee are relished at mid-morning. She plays with her two dogs and grooms them lovingly. She knows that for her, happiness is not dependent upon wealth, success, good health, elaborate pleasures, or possessions. The extent to which Doris is happy now has little to do with what happens *to* her. It is related to an *inner* frame of reference, a choice to go with the goodness of life, no matter what her circumstances.

Brain aneurysms, terminal cancer, AIDS, all have a way of altering perspectives on life. For many, Doris among them, it is the small, simple joys of life that take on renewed meaning and wonder. Yes, Doris has demanding responsibilities; yes, she has considerable stress as a primary caregiver; yes, she is often taxed to her physical and emotional limits. But she can breathe, walk, talk, taste, touch, hear, and feel. She is not yet denied much of life's goodness that she once took for granted. Hollowing out little puff pastries, spooning whipped cream into shells, dusting baked goods with powdered sugar in the early morning hours is but one of the small joys that brings her contentment and a feeling of rightness with life.

Does it have to take a brush with death for us to celebrate the goodness of life regardless of multiple strains and frustrations? No. What it does take is the recognition that we can do more on our behalf to court experiences of quiet happiness.

Over the past twenty years neurosurgeons and neuroscientists have made startling discoveries about the brain from their work with stroke victims and other neurologically impaired people. They have determined the seat of happiness is centered in the left half of the brain entwined with our ability to *think* and make *judgments*.[1]

How we *think* or *judge* a situation has a strong bearing on how we go on to *feel* about it. *Feelings follow thought.* If we judge a situation to be good for us, we feel excited and happy and want to embrace fully the experience. If, however, we judge the same situation to be bad, we either resent the experience or try to move away from it because of the unsettling emotions that the judgment or thoughts trigger.

We make judgments so quickly, so automatically, so unconsciously, that we often are not even aware we have posed the question: "Is this good or bad for me?" Even so, the question always underlies our judgments and determines much of our emotional climate.

Most of us are adept at focusing on all that is wrong in our lives and the world around us. The media continually feeds this tendency. But by constantly dwelling on the negative, we add to whatever stress and discomfort we already have in our lives.

Unquestionably there *is* a lot wrong, both in the outer world and within our own homes. But there are also the cream puffs. Can't we give them equal time? We *do* have a choice. We can, like Doris, decide to love the possibilities for joy in our days.

There is an earthy, practical side to Doris's personality. She recognizes that when she dwells on the unhappy aspects of her life, she feels "lousy." But if she will take the time to sit down in her favorite chair and drink a glass of grape juice, which she pressed from her own grapes, she doesn't feel "lousy"; instead she feels happy to be alive.

Seldom does anyone become a new person overnight. We cannot become infectuously ecstatic about our lives any more than Doris can. But like Doris, we *can* decide daily to take time to enjoy the small, simple pleasures life affords us, small moments of happiness reaching out for us if we will but give them our attention.

The French have an expression for such small precious moments: *le petit moment.* It is "le petit moment" that Doris experiences sitting on her deck awaiting the sunrise, gathering in her grapes, or decorating her home for Christmas. In spite of frustration, discouragement, and weariness, "le petit moment" serves as a reminder of the goodness of life. It is ours for the taking.

"Les petits moments" are as many and varied as we humans can make them: reading aloud to a grandchild, stretching out in a lawn chair in the sun, buttering a cinnamon roll to have with freshly brewed coffee, grooming the cat, making flower arrangements, painting landscapes, painting toenails, singing along with a favorite recording, getting the rings scrubbed out of the bathtub. "Les petits moments" can be sensual like lighting candles as darkness comes on. They can be mental, like working on a crossword puzzle, or becoming absorbed in a good book. They can be the creative dimension of knitting an afghan, or building a bird feeder. They can be the emotional content of sharing a good laugh or a good cry with a friend.

"Les petits moments" cannot be said to be spectacular occurrences by any stretch of the imagination. And yet, when engaged in with thankfulness and joy, they become celebratory reminders of a goodness that underlies and animates life, even in its darkest hours.

Hold onto what is good,
Even if it is a handful of earth.

Hold onto what you believe,
Even if it is a tree that stands by itself.

Hold onto what you must do,
Even if it is a long way from here.

Hold onto life,
Even if it is easier letting go.

Hold onto my hand,
Even when I have gone away from you.

Ancient Pueblo Indian Poem

Caregivers know a lot about holding on. Something deep in our hearts keeps us at our jobs. We know defeat, we know collapse, and we know tears. But somehow most of us manage to hold on.

Cream puffs or no, Doris is not so different from the rest of us. If her limits are exceeded, she breaks. It is then that she shuts herself in her room and cries. There is no shame in her tears; she knows tears are her friends. She is right.

Emotional tears have been found to have a different chemical composition from irritant tears. The tears we shed when we are emotionally upset have significantly more protein than tears caused by irritating substances. Prolactin, a hormone that stimulates milk production in pregnant and nursing women is one of the hormones released in response to stress. Adult women have a 50 to 60 percent higher prolactin level than men, which may explain why women cry more easily and more often then men, with crying being one of the most natural forms of self-medication.[2]

Disruptive emotions have a way of disarming even the most stalwart among us. Anger born of frustration causes us to lash out at those in our care; guilt and self-pity cause us to grow despondent. The anguish of finding ourselves reduced to so much less than we want to be brings with it a host of recriminations. Why did we have to hurt the one we love? Why can't we do a better job of battling discouragement and getting a stronger hold on ourselves?

It is then that tears can come to the rescue. Yes, they relieve tension, but they do more. Our tears serve as poignant reminders of our humanness, part of which will always be emotional fraility in some form or another. Anger, guilt, frustration, and despair are part of being human. Emotional outbursts will occur despite our best efforts.

Sometimes it is more important to forgive ourselves for our failures than to agonize over them. Forgiveness is a reconciling force in life. It allows us our frailities, not to excuse them but to recognize that they are the shadow side of our courage, strength, and compassion. Just as light always casts shadows, to be human is always to err in some capacity of our being.

It is good to learn from failure; it is also good to forgive it and go on with our lives. Doris walks the same emotionally rocky road that all caregivers tread. She may have a keener appreciation of life's goodness than many of us, but that does not keep frustration, futility, and despair from getting the best of her on occasion. Those are the times she shuts herself in her room and cries. Doris welcomes her tears. They serve to remind her that she is human, not superhuman. They also release tension, which allows her to get in touch with her *sources of strength,* ones that, for Doris, are deep within. And although human frailty and moist eyes are not her preferred catalysts for tapping those sources, once tapped, Doris is able to dry her tears and move forward with resolve:

"I knew it wasn't going to be easy. That's the whole point. Once you accept the fact life is going to be difficult, you learn to reach deeper inside you to find ways to keep on keeping on."

NOTES

1. Barry Kaufman, *Happiness Is a Choice* (New York: Fawcett Columbia, 1991).
2. William Frey, *Crying: The Mystery of Tears* (Minneapolis, Minn.: Winston Press, 1985).

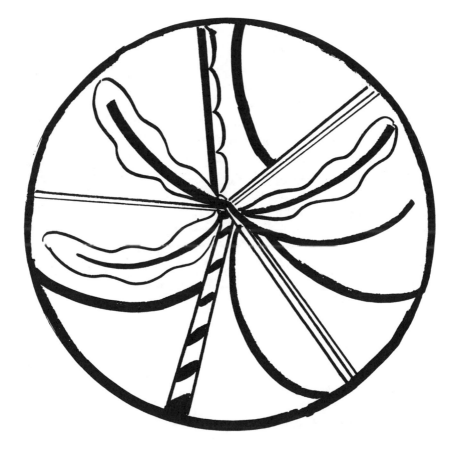

Epilogue

Nothing in life stays static. To everything there *is* a season. *Taking Time for Me* was sixteen months in the writing. As it goes to press, the caregivers whose stories are the heart of this book have yet whole new chapters unfolding in their own lives.

Doris's and Bea's husbands have died. Helen has moved her husband out of institutional care and has returned him to their home to once again become his primary caregiver. Marie has placed her husband in long-term care. Complications at home keep Don from attending the group. Sylvia and Barbara are courting chronic stress-related illnesses. Lisa remains resilient, gathering her strength for the long caregiving years ahead for her. With papers now on file for divorce, Donna begins a new and painful episode in her caregiving journey.

Each member's needs for the others have changed in degree and shifted in scope. The group continues to meet. One or two new faces have appeared. Three or four old faces have dropped away. Although the group has not evolved into a supportive "community"* in the way several members had hoped, meetings continue to serve as welcome events where sorrows can be shared, pent-up emotions released, and where care for one another is experienced as genuine and compassionate.

The intent on the part of some of the group's members to expand its outreach to caregivers throughout the community did not materialize. Stronger professional leadership would be required to do so. The caregivers themselves are mostly too worn from their responsibilities to be able to take the initiative required to broaden their base.

Even so, these Portland caregivers have made more of a contribu-

---

*See page 129.

tion to fellow caregivers than they yet realize. Their willingness to open their lives and their hearts so publicly for outreach in a book may ultimately be of more benefit to larger numbers of caregivers than had they been able to expand the scope of their group.

Because most of us who give care live so cut off from meaningful interaction with other caregivers, we fail to recognize how common the unsettling emotions and experiences we must bear are to caregiving. The truth is, very few of us are appreciably different in any way from Marie, Doris, Bea, and others of the Portland caregivers. We agonize over our guilt feelings. We cry alone in our bedrooooms. We balance precariously between doing too much for our family member and doing not enough.

All such struggles are part of the universal caregiving dilemma. They seem, however, more unsettling when we are not around other caregivers enough to recognize their universality. How much more reassuring it would be if there was a Sylvia living two doors down, or a Helen on the next block. The irony is, there is a great likelihood there *are* caregivers nearby, but unless local churches, social service agencies, senior centers, and care facilities sponsor caregiver support groups, we may never be introduced to them.

What we can do on our own, however, is obtain listings of support groups organized around particular diseases, such as a local Parkinson's Support Group or a local Alzheimer's Support Group. These listings are usually available through local hospitals, the Information and Referral Department of United Way agencies, and through Senior Centers. Even though programs will primarily be about coping with the illness or disease specific to the group, meeting will still provide opportunities to be in contact with other caregivers, establish commonalities of experience, and share resources.

Should support group involvement of any kind not be possible for any number of legitimate reasons, there will be all the more gratitude for the caregivers who shared their lives so willingly for purposes of this book. We who give care do not need heroines or heroes to look up to. We need to exercise a greater appreciation of the heroism in our own caregiving lives. Just as the caregivers in this book are, in their everyday humanness, candidates for admiration, so are the rest of us who place our lives in service to the needs of others. Resentments, frustrations, and recriminations will remain a part of caregiving. But they can't diminish the altruism and great depth of compassion and concern which are the hallmarks of our common caregiver heritage. The caregiver journey can never be an easy one; yet never was there a journey of which anyone can be more proud.

Unfortunately, that pride, which is rightfully ours, has a way of dissipating when we are tired, overworked, deprived of healthy relationships, and worn down from lack of appreciation and/or minimal encouragement from others to keep on with our job. Under such circumstances, **it is only by taking time for ourselves** that we can find the renewed energy to return to our tasks with the care, dedication, and inner strength that bring us to the job in the first place.

This book does not claim to be an exhaustive source of renewal suggestions. What it does claim is unrelenting advocacy for placing the highest priority on meeting caregiver needs for well-being, self-esteem, solidarity, and worth in the community. Whether or not our value is acknowledged by the public, caregiving is as important and honorable a work as any that can be named. We may not be able to command the help that we need or the recognition we deserve. But by taking better care of ourselves *and* one another, we will fare better in keeping our spirits intact and our dedication unswerving.

Index